TEMPTING LITTLE TEASE

THE BLACKWELL-LYON SERIES

**"Entertaining-Light Hearted-Sexy-Adventurous and Fun!!" -** *The Guide To Romance Novels*

"Where are we really going?" I ask.

"Away from Reg. I figured that was enough."

"I could kiss you right now," I tell her, in response to which she tilts her head up.

"Do," she says. "He's watching."

Unlike earlier, I don't hesitate. Earlier was bonus content. This is the actual show, and I take her into my arms, then use my finger to lift her chin as I close my mouth over hers. I'm planning on sensual and romantic. A solid show-kiss for a mixed audience.

But things don't always go the way they're planned. Her lips part, her mouth opening wide to me, and I don't even hesitate. I claim it hungrily, reveling in the way our tongues war and our teeth clash as she clutches the back of my head and pulls me tighter against her. This is more than a kiss, it's a full-on sensual assault, and I feel the effects of it burning through me, heating my blood, firing my senses.

deepest kiss

entice me

hold me

please me

indulge me

# TEMPTING LITTLE TEASE

J. KENNER

A man is nothing without a code.

And he's less than nothing if he breaks his own code.

That's what my father always told me, and with his chest full of medals and an office papered with commendations, General Christopher Anthony Palermo knew a thing or two about honor.

I like to think that I do, too.

My whole life, I've walked the straight and narrow, following but never crossing those lines in the sand. The lines called trust and ethics and good old-fashioned decency.

I respect the law and the system. I don't break my friends' trust or toy with a woman's heart. I don't stand by doing nothing when I see injustice, and I'm willing to get my hands dirty for something I believe in.

I won't stand for being used, and I don't tolerate those who prey on misfortune. I fight fair, but anyone who comes after me or mine better expect to get knocked down.

School. War. Work. Family. Doesn't matter. I've held fast to those tenets my entire life.

Then she slips into my bed, and suddenly I can't keep my code without breaking my code. Around her, everything I know about my life and myself flips completely upside down.

And I honestly can't even tell if that's a bad thing, or something very, very good.

# CHAPTER ONE

"IN OTHER WORDS, you stopped this thief with your ass." Brody Carrington grins at me. "I'm impressed, Leo. You always were resourceful."

"What can I say? I go the extra mile for my clients."

He holds out his beer bottle. "To Leonardo Vincent Palermo. Fastest ass in the West."

I raise mine in response, then clink. "Aw, shucks," I drawl. "You'll make me blush."

He laughs, then takes a long swallow. We're drinking Loaded Coronas, a specialty drink at The Fix on Sixth, a favorite Austin bar that's just a few blocks from my office.

My best friend, Brody Carrington was the first client I brought over to Blackwell-Lyon Security after I started working there about six months ago, and last night I was working a case he'd referred to us.

Simple enough, really. The client was Brody's friend, the right hand of one of the United States' senators from Texas. The Senator's ramping up for re-election, and he suspected that there was someone on his staff selling his secrets and strategies.

It only took a few weeks to confirm the breach and finger the thief. The team and I outlined a plan. We had the Senator plant some cheese, and I lurked in the darkened office, waiting for our rat.

Of course, none of us expected that the rat would break a fifth floor window and try to escape by shimmying down the drainpipe. And since I'm nothing if not devoted to my work, I took off after him, leaping onto the pipe myself, then loosened my grip about halfway down so that I'd slide the rest of the way fast enough to catch him.

To be clear, I hadn't actually planned to knock the prick unconscious with my butt, but you can't argue with success. And I'll be sure to thank my trainer the next time he loads up the barbell for a fresh set of squats. Buns of steel. That's me.

"That's twice you've come through for me." Brody takes a long swig of his drink, then asks, "Want to try for three out of three?"

I lean back in my chair, chuckling. "You've got another job? Brody, my friend, you're attracting assholes like flies."

"Nah, this one's a gimme. Seriously. Pure escort duty, nothing more."

"I can't believe I'm turning down the chance to take you to the prom, my friend, but I've been going non-stop for months. I'm taking a couple of weeks for some R and R."

"Yeah? Where are you heading?"

"Not far. Just South Austin and my house. I've been in this town almost half a year, and the garage is still full of boxes."

He shakes his head in mock reproach. "You are a sad specimen, my friend. Where's your sense of adventure?"

"I get enough adventure on the job," I remind him. "To be honest, I'd originally planned to head up to Dallas and see my folks, but Mom talked Dad into one of those Alaskan cruises." My mother loves to travel, but Dad says he saw enough of the world bouncing all over it during his years in the service. Now, he just wants to stay at home, spending time with his friends, the dogs, and the woman he adores.

He loves my mom too much to stick to his guns, though. And they compromised with Alaska. "Because a cruise is the only way to go to multiple destinations without having to repack your damn suitcase," he'd told me.

"He'll enjoy it," Brody says. "That was the last trip Karen and I took."

"I'm sorry," I say, feeling like an ass. "I didn't know. I wouldn't have mentioned Alaska at all if—"

"I know. It's fine. And it's a good memory. There will always be things that remind me of her. And one of these days, the memories will be happy." He lifts his beer bottle with a shrug. "At least that's what everyone tells me."

I flounder a bit, wishing I had some way to erase the sorry from my friend's eyes. Karen passed away just over three years ago, the victim of a late diagnosed brain tumor. The speed with which she had declined had been a blessing and a curse. She suffered less, but Brody barely had time to wrap his head around what was happening before she was gone.

A few months later, he'd quit his job as a detective with the Dallas Police Department to take over as CEO of the family business after his father retired. He's consistently said that he made the switch for his dad, but I have my own theories. I think he loved his work so much that it was a painful, daily reminder of how much he'd loved Karen. And how much he'd lost when she passed away.

I also think he regrets leaving, though he'll probably never admit it. Brody's not the desk jockey type. Nor does he like playing office politics. So far, though, he's shown no sign that he's thinking about pulling up stakes.

"You've got that apologetic look in your eye," he chides me. "Seriously, it's okay. Buy the next round and hear me out about this job, and we'll call it even."

"Fair enough," I say, then signal for Eric, the bartender, to send over another round.

"You remember Sam, right?"

"Sure," I say, smiling at the memory of his kid sister. "Remember ninth grade? She was, what? In sixth? I thought your mom was going to skin us alive when she learned we ordered Sam to do all your chores so you could come over to my house." The very well-built Myers twins lived behind my house, and my room had an excellent view of their pool.

"It was worth it, though," Brody said. "I wonder what the twins are up to these days..."

"I haven't thought about them in years. Sam, either, to tell you the truth. I don't think I've seen her since we graduated."

Technically Brody's stepsister, Samantha Watson had moved in with Brody when her mom married Brody's dad. She was two and he was five. By the time I met Brody freshman year, there was nothing "step" about their relationship; they were siblings, through and through, and he was the big brother who both harassed and looked after his kid sister. She'd been a gawky pre-teen, and I don't think I ever saw her when she wasn't either buried in a book or a computer game.

And since Brody and I were as close as brothers, Sam became my pseudo-sister, complete with arguments and teasing and sass.

She was a good kid with a snarky sense of humor, and the fact that she needs help from a guy who works in the security business worries me.

"No, no," Brody says when I tell him as much. "Nothing like that. She needs an escort to a wedding."

"That's it?"

Brody shrugs. "I told you it was no big deal. She was planning on going stag, then she found out her ex is going to be there. She's—well, honestly, she wants to go with someone who'll pretend to be her fiancé."

I sit back, amused. "She trying to make this guy jealous?"

"No, no. Unless she's totally bullshitting me, she's not interested in him anymore. But I guess he said some nasty things when they broke up and she wants to take him down a peg. Show him that he was just a stepping stone to the real thing."

He holds up his hands as if in surrender. "It's stupid game-playing, but Sam doesn't date much, and this guy hurt her. It's not socially acceptable for me to beat him up in a dark alley, so I decided I'd back her plan."

"And rope me in," I add with a smile.

"That was her idea, buddy, not mine."

"Really?" A waiter I haven't seen before delivers our second round, and I take a long swallow, enjoying the burn from that first hit of rum filling the neck of the bottle. "Why?"

Brody shrugs. "I'm guessing it's because you're the second best thing to me."

I raise my brows, and he laughs. "I mean that she's not looking for a fling, just someone who'll play the part. Obviously, she can't drag along her real brother, so she wants the runner-up."

"A guy she can trust."

He nods. "She always thought of you as safe, but she doesn't know you like I do." He spreads his hands, as if asking *what can you do?*

I cross my arms over my chest, trying not to let Brody rankle me. Especially since he speaks the truth.

"I promised her I'd ask. But dammit, Leo, don't agree unless you can handle the job. And by that I mean not handling my sister."

Anger flares inside me, red and ripe. "Pull it back a notch," I say, my voice low and edging toward dangerous. I can see in his eyes that he knows he pushed me a little too close to the line. "Do you really think I'd go there?"

For a moment, we just look at each other. Two men who know each other better than most brothers, and sometimes that can be a dangerous thing. For a moment, it seems as if the whole bar has fallen silent. Then Brody shakes his head. More of a twitch, really, but it's enough. Then tension shatters like glass, and we both pick up our bottles.

"Fuck, man," he says. "She's my kid sister."

"She's an adult now," I remind him. "And I am, too."

He cocks his head and says nothing.

I lift my upper lip. "Asshole. I may not be a monk, but I can keep it in my pants when I want to."

"Can? Or will?"

"What the fuck, Brody?" I mean, come on. Brody's supposed to be my best friend. Which, I guess, does mean he knows me better than anybody. So maybe his concerns are legitimate.

Or maybe they're not. Lately, I've gotten a bit tired of riding the hook-up train. I haven't fucked a woman in over two months. And I'm not sure if I'm getting bored with the whole damn thing, or if I'm just ready to settle down.

Honestly, both options scare the shit out of me.

"What?" I say, realizing that Brody's been rattling on about something.

"I said I'm sorry. I was being an ass. But she's my sister, so just promise me, okay? Make me feel better about asking you this, because I swear I'm only doing it because Sam asked me to. I know you, man."

"If you did, you'd know there's no way in hell I'd make a pass. She's like a little sister to me, too."

"So is that a yes? I can tell her you're in for this crazy scheme?"

I shake my head, not in response, but in bewilderment. "Crazy is right. Honestly, Bro, it's a little off the wall."

"Can't argue with that, but if you get past the crazy, it sounds like a great deal. It's a destination wedding. A long weekend in Fredericksburg," he adds, referring to a charming town in the Texas Hill Country that has become famous for its local vineyards, restaurants, and shopping. "Go up Friday. Come back Monday morning after the wedding. You drink. You eat. You sit around and read. You've been going a million miles an hour since you moved to Austin, right? And you can unpack anytime. How often do you get the chance to go on an all-expense paid vacation where the alcohol is included?"

It's a fair point. And I've been managing just fine without all the crap that's still in those boxes.

"Remember her freshman formal right before we graduated?" he prompts.

I scowl. "Now you're playing dirty." She'd worn a denim jumper over a long-sleeve T-shirt and Doc Martin shoes. A more confident girl could have pulled it off, but Sam was the geeky, shy girl.

I never knew exactly what happened that night, but when she couldn't track down her parents or Brody, she'd called me, begging me to come pick her up. I did. I'd taken her home, but not before taking her into the center of the gym for one dance. It had been a slow song—Aerosmith's *I Don't Want To Miss A Thing* —and she'd practically shaken in my arms as everyone watched us.

Then I kissed her, walked her off the dance floor, and took her to Whataburger for fries and a shake.

"You were like her knight," Brody says. "A knight who flipped off the rest of the freshman class."

"She was a good kid who didn't deserve to be teased."

"True that," Brody says. "She was such a gawky thing back then."

"From what I saw last Halloween on your feed, she still is." I'm rarely on social media, so I miss a lot, but from what I can tell, Sam hardly ever posts pictures. Or maybe Brody just never shares them. Last year, though, he'd shared one of her posts after a Halloween party.

Honestly, she'd looked pretty much the same. Adorable, but gawky.

Brody chuckles. "I forget you haven't seen her since senior year. But seriously, you changed her life that night. Because of you, she had a much better sophomore year. People remembered that hot shit Leo Palermo was her date that night. It mattered."

I suppose it did. By senior year, I was definitely up there in the high school social strata. I was into sports, made solid grades, and was on the Student Council. Plus, it didn't hurt that I've got my dad's dark, Italian looks and a decent build.

"You know, that formal was the last time I saw her." I'd gone to college out of state, and by the time I moved back to Texas, she was in Seattle working at some video game company. "Has it really been that long?"

"Time flies," Brody says. "Remember after you brought her home? I'd just pulled up from a date with somebody, and she told me what happened and how you were her hero, and I said—"

"That one or the other of us would always be there for her. I remember."

"And then we went off to college and abandoned her," Brody adds. "Pretty shitty of us really."

"Is this your way of guilting me into helping her now?"

"Hell, yes."

I have to laugh. "Okay, give me her phone number. I'm not saying yes, but I'll at least get her take on this scam."

"You should talk to her in person."

"When's she flying in for this shindig?"

"She's not," he says. "She's already here."

## CHAPTER TWO

ACCORDING TO BRODY, Sam came to Austin to
do contract work for some video game company. She's
staying in Crestview, an established neighborhood in
the heart of Austin with charming bungalows and lots
of shade trees. It's one of my favorite areas, and I'd
looked to buy there before finally renting south of the
river. When my lease is up, I'll look again. In the
meantime, considering I still haven't unpacked, I think
I'm done with moving.

I find the rather bedraggled one-story house easily
enough, then pull up beside the curb since a baby blue
Mini Cooper is already in the driveway, parked in front
of the detached one-car garage. The door is up, and as I
come closer, I see at least a dozen paint cans scattered
about, as well as an interior door balanced on top of
two sawhorses.

I follow a buckling sidewalk through the front yard to the concrete stairs that lead to a wooden porch painted in brown, peeling paint.

I pull open the screen door, knock a couple of times, and wonder if I'll even recognize her.

A moment later, the door flies open, and I'm staring at Samantha Watson's wide, happy grin. Her dark brown hair is pulled back beneath a blue bandana, and there's a white streak of paint on her cheek that makes me think of street urchins. She's at least three inches taller than the last time I saw her, the top of her head now reaching my chin.

In my mind, she's still built like a pre-teen fence post, but to be fair, I can't get any real sense of her figure since she's wearing a paint-splattered men's button-down that doubles as a smock and baggy, faded jeans.

I can see her face just fine, though. The same, but different. Her wide brown eyes seem bigger and darker, with the kind of lashes that Cayden's wife Gracie wears when she's modeling, but on Sam are the real deal. The childish round face that's burned into my memories has given way to a perfect oval accented by cheekbones that stand out when she smiles. Something she's doing right now, actually, and I can't help but notice that her plump lips and wide mouth were made for smiling. And for other things. Things that I have no business noticing about my best friend's sister. Not even in passing. Not even casually.

I'm still lecturing myself when she steps forward, obviously intending to give me a hug. And, damn me, I actually take a step back, her lush lips still filling my vision and Brody's all-too-strict warning still ringing in my ears.

To my relief, she laughs. "I know. Awkward, right? I mean, you were like my brother, but it's been ages. Probably best to start out with a friendly handshake and work our way up to social hugging."

She thrusts out her hand, and I take it, noticing how well it fits into mine, and surprised at how smooth her skin is despite the fact that she apparently spends a lot of time working with her hands.

"From what Brody tells me," I say, "we won't be stopping at the social hug."

It might be my imagination, but I think her grip tightens slightly. Not that I have time to analyze the nuances of our connection, because she gently tugs her hand free.

She clears her throat, then steps aside and ushers me into the house. "Listen, thank you so much. I know this whole thing must sound crazy, and I can't even tell you how much it means to me that you agreed to do it."

"I didn't—"

"I know. Brody told me the whole story about how

you didn't want to, but then you remembered how you two pledged to look out for me. And even though I'm old enough to look out for myself now, I really, really appreciate this."

She pauses, looking me over once more before she shuts the front door and gestures me further into the house.

I hesitate, because this is the moment when I should tell her that I need to leave so that I can go strangle her brother. The guy never could keep a secret.

"It's not that I didn't want to help..." I trail off lamely as she flashes me a crooked smile.

"I believe you. Why wouldn't you want to go off to Fredericksburg to a weekend wedding hosted by people you've never met with a woman you haven't seen since she was a kid, but now you'll have to pretend to be her fiancé even though you don't even know her favorite color?"

"When you put it that way, I must be crazy." I flash a faux salute, then start to turn toward the door. "See ya."

Her laughter fills the room, and when she grabs hold of my arm and pulls me back, I'm grinning, too. "Hold on there, cowboy. You already signed onto this rodeo. I'm not letting you get away so easily."

She's still holding my arm. But right then, I'm not inclined to alter that particular status quo.

"I'm just saying that I appreciate it." Her words are soft and heartfelt.

"Like I was trying to say earlier, I want to help. And as for that other thing..."

"Other thing?"

"Green," I say. "Your favorite color is green."

I can see the surprise in the way her eyebrows scrunch. She always did have the most expressive face of any girl I'd ever known.

"What?" I tease. "Did you think you were that forgettable?"

She shoves her hands into the pockets of her paint-splattered jeans, her shoulders and brows rising and falling together. "Well, I hoped not," she says, more to the carpet than to me. "But I'm still impressed."

When she lifts her head, her cheeks seem a bit pinker, and I'm struck by just how well the parts that make up Samantha Watson fit together. And by the fact that she's no longer the little girl I used to know.

On the contrary, Samantha Watson's all grown up.

"Yeah, well, that summer is burned into my mind for a lot of reasons."

She nods. "That was the summer you met Brody."

"And you followed us around for a month begging him to help you paint your room green."

"I had to. I was a damsel in distress. Mom and Dad thought it was a terrible idea, but I was certain that when they saw it, they'd be impressed. So I figured I needed it done all at once."

"Which meant you needed help." I shake my head, remembering how she'd stood on the steps, hands on her hips, and made her case. "I can't believe we agreed."

"*We?*" She cocks her head. "Brody said no. It was only after you said that we could each pull a trailer on our bikes and go to the hardware store for the paint that he got into the idea. That was very cool of you, by the way. I always thought so."

I grin as I follow her through the small living area and into a spacious kitchen that more or less resembles a war zone. "Yeah, well, I'll tell you a secret. Brody may have thought the whole thing was a joke, but I felt like some sort of hero helping you out that way."

Two stools are tucked in under a bar-height counter, which, at the moment, is constructed only of plywood. She raps lightly on the wood. "This'll be stunning once I get the countertop in," she says as I take a seat, and she moves on to the refrigerator. "And just so you know, you *were* my hero that day." She opens the fridge and holds out a bottle of white wine, one articulate brow rising in question. I nod, and she pours two glasses. "To my hero of yesteryear," she says, raising her glass in a toast. "And to my hero this weekend. I guess that makes you two for two."

Her words are light, almost casual, but she's looking right at me, and damned if my whole body doesn't feel warm. Then I notice that she's unbuttoning her shirt, and the warm rush shoots south, making me very glad I'm sitting down. "Uh, Sam. What are you—"

But before I get the rest of my words out, she says, "Sorry about the temperature. The stupid AC has been on the fritz since I bought this place, and the kitchen is the worst." She casually tugs off the shirt, leaving her clad in a scoop neck tank top that reveals some very unexpected curves.

Apparently, Sam really did grow up.

I clear my throat and—in an effort to distract myself from Sam's truly spectacular tits—start to survey the shambles of a kitchen. The open cabinetry is all half-sanded, and doors of every size litter countertops. Everywhere I look, Dixie cups overflow with hinges and screws. Not to the mention the sawdust, paint brushes, and open cans of primer all over the plastic-covered flooring.

"You bought this place?" I ask, her earlier words coming back to me. "Are you moving here? Brody said you were only here for a contract job."

"Yeah," she said. "But this place was a steal, and it's going to be fabulous once I finish. The housing market in Austin is still strong, so I should make a pretty solid profit, especially since I'm doing a ton of the work myself."

I'm impressed, and I tell her as much.

"The place has good bones," she says. "The cabinets are from the forties and they're rock solid. But the paint and pulls are ugly as sin. So I'm redoing them one at a time. And this," she adds, smacking the heel of her hand on the plywood that is serving as a countertop, "will be gone just as soon as the new countertops come in. Composite glass," she adds. "It's going to look amazing."

"It will," I agree, looking around the room with fresh eyes, trying to see it the way she obviously does. "Won't it be hard to part with?"

She shrugs. "I came here to tackle one specific project. Well, one I planned, and one bonus project that just sort of fell into my lap. And that's all great, but my career's back in Seattle."

"That doesn't answer my question."

"No, I guess it doesn't." She takes a long sip of wine, then leans back against the sink, her back arched so that her tank pulls tight against her breasts, and I come close to absolutely losing my shit.

She looks me in the eye, then nods. The slightest, most minuscule nod ever. "Yes," she says, her voice almost a whisper. "I think it will be hard to part with.

But I didn't come to Austin with any long term expectations."

"You came for the gaming project, and all this is just a perk."

"But a hell of a perk."

"I thought all you made were digital weapons and imaginary cities," I tell her. "I had no idea you were so handy in the real world."

I sip my wine, realizing that I don't really know Samantha Watson at all. Not any more. Now, she's fascinating and talented and easy on the eyes. She's everything she was and yet so much more. And for one sharp moment, I wonder if this weekend is a huge mistake.

"You sound like Brody. He thinks that just because I work in the gaming world that I live there, too." She tilts her head, and I get the feeling she's studying me. "What do you mean, 'you thought'? Mr. Palmero, have you been checking up on me over the years?"

"Sure," I admit. "Brody brags about how well you're doing in the gaming world all the time. And I've asked him for a few updates, too."

"Yeah?" Her smile is so bright, I'm glad I confessed to keeping tabs. "Gone but not forgotten, huh?"

"Never," I assure her, then feel my breath catch in my throat when she holds my gaze, her face alight with pleasure. For a moment, we just stand like that, my head filled with the rush of my own blood pounding through my body.

With any other woman, I'd take this up a notch. See if the electricity crackling between us is my imagination or if there's some genuine chemistry brewing. And if so, I'd jump right back on the hook-up train and gleefully break my two-month celibacy streak.

But Sam isn't any other woman. She's Brody's sister, and he'd have my balls for breakfast.

Since I'm rather fond of my current anatomical state, I clear my throat, and glance sharply away, focusing on the room around us instead of the woman in front of me. "You're really doing all of this on your own? Have you done it before?"

"I volunteered for Habitat for Humanity in Seattle, and then helped out a few friends with remodels. A couple of them have since moved here—it's a good market for the gaming community—so they've popped in a couple of times to see my progress."

"They're not reciprocating? Not helping you out with all of this?"

She raises a shoulder. "I like doing things on my own. It's ..." She trails off, as if searching for the right word. "Relaxing. No, strike that. It's familiar."

I almost ask what she means, but then realize that I

don't need to, because the memories are flooding back. Samantha floating in her family's pool by herself. Samantha, fixing up her bike on her own, despite Brody and me both volunteering to help. Samantha, walking to school on her own, headphones in as she marched to her own beat, while Brody drove the battered Subaru wagon that had been his pride and joy junior and senior year.

She'd always been a loner. I think that's one of the reasons I'd been so moved by her misery at that dance. I never thought that the other kids' opinions mattered that much to her.

Or maybe I just hadn't thought at all.

"Well, if you change your mind, I'd be happy to help you work on the house."

For a moment, she simply looks at me, her face blank. Then a wide smile spreads across her face. "You know what? I think I'd really like that." She indicates the rest of the house with a wave of her hand. "Want the grand tour?"

"Sure."

It's a small house—about twelve hundred square feet, but the back patio off the kitchen is large and screened in. There's a ping-pong table there, which she tells me was left over by the former owners, along with an old-fashioned tire swing that hangs from a giant oak in the back yard.

"It's a mess," she says, nodding at the overgrown yard. "But I'll get it under control eventually."

There are two entrances to the patio, the second one being through the master bedroom. It's a simple square room with nothing more than a mattress and box spring on a metal frame and a chest of drawers. The attached bathroom is in desperate need of updating, and Sam tells me that's the part she's most looking forward to. "Of course, I'll have to hire a plumber, but it will be worth it to have a walk-in shower and a clawfoot tub. Bathrooms add the most value, you know."

The second bedroom is across the hall from the master, and it's set up as her office. "Eventually, I'll redo this room as a bedroom," she tells me. "But until then, this is where the magic happens. Unless I'm having one of those days. In which case, this is where the frustration happens."

"Days when you can't figure out whether the ogre needs a sword or a mace?"

"You know, it's been a long time since any of my games have included an ogre," she says. "But I'll remember that for the next time I get stuck. Even if it's a racing game. I'll just stick an angry ogre in the middle of the track and give him a sword."

"I think you're on to something," I say, and we both laugh.

"Not a problem you have working security, I guess," she continues. "Getting stuck, I mean. Not ogres."

"Well, there are definitely a few ogres in my line of work. As for getting stuck, I end up spinning my wheels more than I like to admit, trying to figure out where to look next for information or how to best tackle a problem."

She pauses at the end of the hall in front of the large open area that serves as both the home's entrance and the living room. "Sometimes the best way is to go undercover, right?"

"Sure."

She nods, as if considering something. "So what problems do you have on your plate right now?"

"Nothing at the moment," I admit.

"Good." She tilts her head to the side as she studies me. "That must mean you know exactly how to play the role of my fiancé."

That slow burn eases into my gut again, and I gamely ignore it. "I think I can wing it."

The corner of her mouth tugs up, revealing a small dimple in the cheek with the paint. "I bet you can."

I clear my throat, certain I'm imagining the heat in her voice. "So your ex—he's not the groom?"

"Oh, no. Reg is another guest. A cousin of the

bride, who happens to be one of my best friends. Who knew?"

I frown as I mentally follow that web in my mind. "Best friend? Does that mean you're actually in the wedding?"

She shakes her head. "No. She has two sisters, so the bride's side is entirely a family affair. But Becca and I were tight in college, so I'm definitely going to help out when I can. Which means you should get lots of downtime to chill by the pool or go into town or whatever. That's a perk, right?"

"Right," I say automatically, surprised by how much the thought of not spending the entire weekend with her bothers me. I tell myself that it's only because I won't know another soul at this shindig, and force my mind onto another topic. "So tell me about him. If we're engaged, I should know about your ex, right?"

"Right. Well, we both worked for MT-Tech in Seattle. It's a German-based company with a huge online gaming division. He was an assistant project manager and I was doing contract work on one specific game while I tried to get my own company off the ground. At first we just worked together, then we realized we both grew up in Texas and started hanging out more. Friends at first, then..."

She trails off with a shrug.

"And then it was good," I continue for her. "And then it went bad."

"That pretty much sums it up. Now he's dating Lisa Bronwyn. You know the name?"

I shake my head.

"Her dad's Arwin Bronwyn. He's the owner of MT's biggest competitor, Sunspot Entertainment."

"That one I've heard of. It's based in Austin, right?"

"Yup. Reg works there now and word on the street is that he's the golden boy because of some terrifically innovative product he's going to bring in-house, and that Bronwyn is so impressed that he's going to make Reg the vice-president in charge of the entire online gaming division by next year."

"In other words, your ex—Reg?—dumped you and is trying to sleep his way up in the world."

Her brows arch and rise. "I know it's shallow of me to even care if he notices who I'm with, but it burns me that he was using me, and tossed me aside when I was no longer useful."

"Not shallow," I say. "But probably unnecessary. I'm sure you can do a hell of a lot better."

Her smile lights up the room, and she surprises me by taking my hands and easing her body up against mine. "Of course I can," she says, her voice low and a little breathy. "I'm engaged to you, aren't I?"

I tense, suddenly keenly aware of the swell of her breasts against my chest. "Sam..." I swallow, my body reacting in all sorts of ways it really shouldn't be reacting.

"I know, I know. It's only...." She licks those kissable lips. "It's just that I really want him to believe we're real. If he realizes it's all fake, he'll spread the word, and I'll look like an idiot from Austin to Seattle and beyond. *Shit*."

The sharp word is underscored with motion as she lurches out of my arms. "I'm so, so sorry. Crap. This was a stupid idea. I'm a total idiot. It's not fair to you, and—"

Without thinking, I take her hand, pull her hard against me, and claim that gorgeous mouth for my own. At first, she's stiff in my arms. Then she melts against me, and she feels so damn perfect that I can't help but think that I'm the one who's the idiot, not her. Because she'd given me the opportunity to back away slowly. Instead, I not only walked through the door, I damned near did a handspring over the threshold.

I pull away, then shake my head sternly in response to the question painted all over her beautiful, dazed face. "We're not calling it off, and I can play the part. Don't you remember all those shows I did in junior high and high school?"

I don't know why I add the last. Maybe because we

both need to be clear what's happening here. We're putting on a show for Reg. But there's nothing real about it. Not a single goddamn thing.

"You're sure?" She drops her gaze, her lashes dark against her pale skin. "You'll need to act like you want me desperately. If Reg doesn't believe that an incredibly hot, sexy guy has completely flipped over me, then there's no point to this whole charade."

If I were a smarter man, I'd take the out she's offering. Instead I say, "Of course, I'll do it."

"Thank you. You really are the best." She rises onto her tiptoes and kisses the corner of my mouth. A sweet gesture. Tender. Nothing sexual at all.

But that doesn't stop every part of my body from stiffening with both heat and awareness.

Every. Part. Of. My. Body.

That's the moment I realize how excruciatingly hard it's going to be to keep my promise to Brody—and that I really, *really* should have said no.

# CHAPTER THREE

"I THINK IT'S SWEET," Gracie says, aiming her photogenic smile at me first and then the rest of the group gathered in the spacious kitchen of the Northwest Austin house she shares with her husband Cayden.

The comment is in response to my review of my changed plans for the weekend. Specifically, that I'm going to play the part of a besotted fiancé instead of spending the days unpacking and organizing my sadly ignored little house.

"Don't you think it's sweet?" Gracie asks Cayden when no one else answers. With his tousled black hair and his familiar eye patch, he looks a bit like a pirate. He slides in behind her and rests his hands over her lower belly. "I love you, babe," he murmurs to her. "But that is not a recipe for sweet."

Her blond hair fans out as she whirls in his arms and pretends to smack him. At the same time, Connor, Cayden's identical twin, snorts out a laugh from the other side of the massive kitchen island.

Cayden ignores his brother, grabs Gracie's wrist, and pulls her close for a kiss. She melts against him, and when they part, he's smiling at her. "Love you, wife," he says.

Cayden lost his eye in Afghanistan, and had a rough time of it after. In addition to the eye, his first wife was apparently a piece of work. I didn't know the woman, but I can't imagine him with anyone other than Gracie.

Her lips twitch with amusement ... or possibly irritation. "Love you, too, husband. Although I'm not sure how much stock you should put into that. After all, I'm not too bright."

"Zing!" Kerrie says, coming around the island with two glasses of red wine. She hands one to Cayden, then holds out the other for me.

"I can wait," I say as I nod toward Gracie, who shakes her head.

"Take it," she says. "I'm fine with water."

"You sure?" Connor asks, holding the bottle as he pours another two glasses. "It's a celebration. There aren't many cases that close so uniquely," he adds with a glance in my direction.

I raise my wine in a mock toast. "Brody already made all the ass jokes. But I'm still happy to celebrate."

"I am, too," Gracie says. "That's why my water is fizzy."

"You're going to float away," Connor says. "That's all you drink lately."

Gracie's blue eyes sparkle as she smiles. "I'm working this week. And your skin looks better for the camera when you just drink water."

Connor shrugs, looking nonplussed. Cayden, on the other hand, is practically beaming. I tilt my head and pretend to look at my wine so as to hide my grin. Connor's an excellent investigator, but on this score he's failed. Even so, I think he'll be an outstanding uncle. And sooner or later, he'll get a clue.

Despite the fact that the house is huge, we continue to linger in the kitchen, and I take my wine to the farm-style breakfast table, then sit back and watch my friends, feeling pretty damn lucky.

I met Cayden back when we were both in the service, and we hit it off. So much so that he eventually asked me to consider joining Blackwell-Lyon Security. I'd been working private security for years, but for a huge company where I felt like just one more cog in an endlessly turning wheel of billable hours and deathly dull assignments.

Cayden and Connor make up the Lyon part of

Blackwell-Lyon, and Pierce Blackwell makes up the rest. And though I didn't know Pierce well before starting the job, he's become a solid friend, too. Tonight, he's in Los Angeles with his wife, Jez, whose sister is getting some television award. Not an Emmy, but other than that I haven't got a clue. But Jez is thrilled, which means I am, too.

The most excited person in the room about Del's award is Kerrie, Pierce's younger sister and Connor's fiancée. Were it not for the fact that she's deep in wedding planning—and has plenty of work piled up as the Blackwell-Lyon office manager—I'm sure she would have tried to wrangle a ticket. Unlike me, she not only knows the name of the award, but also what movie—or maybe TV show?—it's for.

I watch Kerrie in her skinny jeans and T-shirt, her dark blond hair bouncing in a ponytail, my mind wandering to Sam. She's not that much older than Kerrie, and even though she doesn't work in Hollywood, she's definitely in the entertainment industry. *She* probably knows what award Del is getting, too.

I frown, and for the first time realize that I haven't got the faintest idea what's in store for me this weekend. Sam was easy to talk to as a kid, but what do we have in common now? Generally, when I'm out with a woman, I keep a mental list of neutral topics handy for cocktail or dinner talk. After that, as per my usual *modus operandi* there's not much talking.

But with Sam, we're going to be together constantly for an entire weekend. And my usual mental list isn't going to hack it.

I cut my thoughts off with a shake of my head, reminding myself that it doesn't matter. We're playing a role. Unscripted, maybe, but we can make it up as we go. And if there are conversational lapses, I'll just wax poetic about some fictional amazing date we had early in our relationship.

All of which is well and good. Or it would be if this was only about the show we're putting on. But it's not. It's about—

"Blue balls," Cayden says, his words and everyone else's laughter pulling me out of my reverie.

They're all looking at me, and I narrow my eyes as I stare Cayden down. "Want to clue me in on the joke?"

"Cayden's being an ass, as usual," Kerrie says, a tease in her voice.

Cayden eyes Connor. "You need to keep your woman under control."

Connor laughs. "You've known her as long as I have. Do you really think that's possible? Besides, my woman is right."

He turns to me as Cayden and Kerrie both start to laugh. "I was just saying that I thought you wanted

down time at your house. A few weeks to catch-up and
relax. But playing lover-boy doesn't sound relaxing.
Especially since you don't get to method act. Honestly,
it sounds seriously stressful."

"Stop it," Gracie says. "He's doing a nice thing for
an old friend."

"See? *Blue balls,*" Cayden says again, this time in a
whisper.

"Gracie's right," I say. "I'm doing Brody—and Sam
—a favor. I'm not looking to score with Samantha
Watson."

Which is the absolute truth. What I don't say is
that I'm undeniably attracted to her, a fact that I've
been coming to terms with since I saw her yesterday.

"Are you sure?" Kerrie says, and I honestly can't
tell if she's teasing or not. "Connor and I finally got
together for real after pretending to be together." She
blows him a kiss, then adds, "The pretending can
definitely up the heat factor."

"I can't believe she's saying this," Connor says.
"Hello, private moments."

"We're engaged, sweetie. I think they all figured it
out."

"What?" Cayden says, deadpan, and we all start
laughing. At least until I hold up my hand to quiet
everyone. Because it's time to put an end to the ribbing
and the speculation. For them, and for me.

"One, Samantha Watson is an old friend. End of story."

"And what?" Cayden chimes in. "You won't convince me that you of all people are opposed to friends with benefits."

"Two," I continue, ignoring my friend, "even if I was tempted to wring some benefits out of the friendship, I wouldn't. She's my best friend's little sister, which is reason enough."

"And if she's the one starting something?" Cayden asks.

"She's not," I say. "She just needs a favor. Stop seeing hidden agendas where there aren't any."

But it's an occupational hazard, and now that he's spoken the words, I can't get the possibility out of my head. In military training, we're taught to run scenarios. But that's not something I want to do. Because I'm pretty damn sure that any scenario that has Samantha throwing herself at me will not end with a PG rating.

"Sorry," Cayden says, and for a second I think that he's seen my thoughts. "I'm just ribbing you. Like you said, it's just a job like any other. No big deal."

"Exactly," I say, but I have to force the word out. "No big deal at all."

# CHAPTER FOUR

HER FRONT DOOR bursts open right as I pull up alongside the curb. Sam steps outside and waves at me, her grin so wide I can almost believe she's been counting the minutes since I left her.

She's wearing a pale blue V-neck T-shirt that accentuates the curves I saw on my last visit, as well as denim shorts that reveal long, athletic legs leading up to straight hips and an ass that doesn't quite fill out the shorts, but suits her build. I can't help but superimpose my memory of gangly young Sam onto the current model, and can't deny that I like the way she's grown-up.

She's not as curvy as the women I'm usually attracted to, but I still wonder what those legs would feel like wrapped tight around me. Then I mentally curse myself for the way forbidden thoughts about Brody's sister keep popping into my head.

She pops back inside, but returns in an instant, tugging her suitcase over the threshold before turning back to pull the door closed and lock it.

By the time she's turning around again, I'm out of the car and hurrying up the buckling sidewalk to meet her.

"Let me," I say, then take the suitcase and haul it down the three concrete stairs.

"I can get it," she protests, still on the porch with a giant leather tote bag slung over her shoulder.

"I don't doubt it." I keep my hand tight on the handle. "But I'm happy to do it for you. Or would you rather I not?"

She hesitates then offers me a small smile. "No. It's nice of you to offer. Thanks."

I return her smile, then tug the case the rest of the way to the curb. I've already opened the hatch remotely, but I leave the case for a moment and detour to open the door for her before hauling the suitcase into the back of my Toyota Highlander.

When I slide in behind the wheel, I notice that her tote is taking up almost all of the floor space in front of her seat. "Want me to put that in the back, too?"

"Nope. This is my treat bag."

"You're sure?" I say as I start the car.

"Yup." She motions to the road. "Ready?"

In response, I pull out onto the street, then mentally calculate the quickest route to Mo-Pac, one of Austin's north-south freeways, and then onto the spider web of state highways that will lead us into the Texas Hill Country.

As I shift in and out of traffic, she leans forward and pulls out a bag of miniature Snickers bars followed by a can of Dr. Pepper, which she shoves into the cup holder on my side of the car. "It's still cold," she says.

I can't help but laugh. "How on earth did you remember that?"

She shrugs. "How could I forget after that drive to Winedale?"

"Good point."

The summer after freshman year of high school, Brody and I drove to Shakespeare at Winedale with Tony Cox, a senior who was our friend for two reasons. One, he had a drivers license. And two, he was cool with Brody's constant care of his little sister—a job that was frequently dumped on him since both his parents traveled for work.

The three of us had been in the same intro to drama class, and the teacher suggested we check out a show and the long-running Winedale workshop. Started in the Seventies by a professor in the English Department at the University of Texas, the program's dedicated to helping students learn more about Shakespeare by publicly performing the works in a small converted barn located in the small town of Winedale, about halfway between Austin and Houston. In the summer, the students in the program actually spend two months on site, living and breathing Shakespeare.

By the time Tony, Brody, and I went, it had been going for decades and decades, so I guess the program was a success. We liked it, too. It was hot as hell, true, but none of us cared. Even Sam enjoyed it. We'd thought she'd be bored out of her mind, but she'd been positively engrossed in the plight of Romeo and Juliet. On the way back, we'd shared the back seat, and she'd quizzed me about true love and made up alternate endings where the hero and heroine didn't die, but instead escaped together for their happily ever after.

During both legs of the trip, we'd stopped multiple times for snacks, and while Tony, Sam, and Brody all rotated their choices, I was DP and Snickers all the way.

"You still like them, I hope."

"Love them," I tell her honestly. "Although since I crossed the thirty marker, I don't indulge much anymore." When I was in the military, I was in such good shape I could eat anything. Now, I'm still in great shape, but that's because I *don't* eat just anything.

"Oh. Right. I forgot you're old and decrepit now."
She pulls a Snickers from the bag, then peels it open.
"Since I'm still young and in my twenties, I can indulge
in whatever I want."

She bites the candy in half, but her eyes are
entirely on me, full of a flirtatious tease.

*Just let it go.* I can practically hear Brody lecturing
me. But she's captured my attention now, and so I
counter with, "I said I don't indulge *much*. But the
truth is, I'm always looking for an excuse to cheat."

"That's exactly what I wanted to hear. And just so
you know, I'm a notorious enabler." And even though
the words are innocent and about snack food, my
imagination gets the better of me, and I hear the low
timbre of seduction in her voice.

*Wishful thinking or preparing for the worst?*

I want to tell myself it's the latter.

I also want to tell myself to turn on the radio.
Anything to counter the electricity in the car
right now.

But I don't.

On the contrary, when she says, "Open," I do just
that. She slips the other half of her Snickers into my
mouth. And right then I know that I'll never look at
that candy the same way again.

"Good?"

"Definitely." My voice is raspier than usual. I

blame the caramel, then force myself to concentrate on the road.

"I'm glad. Just let me now when you want another one."

*Oh, holy Christ.*

I draw in a breath, then take a sip of the soda, thankful when I turn onto Lamar Boulevard because the traffic is a mess, and focusing on the road will keep my thoughts in check.

Except it doesn't work. Because despite the promise I made to my best friend, I can't deny the fantasy that is running through my head in one delicious, sensual loop. A fantasy that I blame Cayden for. Him and his intriguing question: *And if she's the one starting something?*

Damn Cayden and his theories. When I was with Brody just two days ago, I had nothing but platonic thoughts about Sam. Now, though...

Now this entire adventure is going to be far more of a challenge than I'd anticipated.

"I think you should be an actor," she says once she's pulled out her own snacks—Diet Coke and a giant bag of Popcornopolis.

The question pulls me back to the moment. "One, what are you talking about? And two, how come I'm not seeing chocolate on your side of the car?"

"That's your vice. Mine's popcorn. I could live on

the stuff. Remember when we used to go to the movies almost every weekend? Saturday and Sunday, and we'd usually stay for more than one show?"

I chuckle as the memory comes back to me. Brody and I wanted to sit together so that we could share snarky comments—a habit which irritates me now, and for which I now apologize to anyone who ever sat near us. Since Sam didn't like the way Brody slathered on butter and dry cheese topping, she sat on my other side, and we shared a bucket.

"Do you still go to movies?" she asks.

"Not as much. But who does these days, what with streaming and HDTV."

"I do," she admits. "There's too much clutter if you watch a movie in your own house. And I don't mean clothes and junk strewn about. Mind clutter. But if you go into a theater, you're away from home, and the dark engulfs you..." She trails off with a shrug. "You lose yourself for a while, and you come out with a whole new perspective."

I consider that, nodding slowly. "You may be right."

"I am," she assures me. "If I have a problem—work or personal—I always seem to come out of the theater with a solution."

That leads into a discussion of our favorite streaming shows, including a currently popular one that has a time travel element. That, of course, spins us off in an entirely new direction, and by the time we hit Johnson City and make the turn toward Fredericksburg, we've spent over an hour in non-stop conversation about shows and time travel and what we'd do if we met our selves in another time.

"You have to steer clear," I say, because I am a die-hard *Back To The Future* fan. "You can't risk messing something up."

"No, no. Do that, and you're blowing a huge opportunity to sit yourself down and explain what's what. I mean, how incredible would that be? To be able to share what you've learned with your younger self and completely avoid some of your worst mistakes."

"For example?" I prod.

"That hideous perm I got in eleventh grade is high on the list," she says. "That and Reginald Thorne."

"This weekend's Reg? That's his last name? Thorne?"

"That's him." She shifts in her seat, then reaches into the popcorn bag. "Why? Do you know him?"

"No. Just thinking about his last name. He's not the devil, is he?"

When she grins, I know she gets the reference to *The Omen*. "Well, *I* think so. But I doubt he's going to cause Armageddon. He's really not that important."

"Glad to hear it. I'm not sure I'm the kind of guy who can make the devil jealous."

"Oh, you most definitely are." This time, there is no denying the sensual tone in her voice, and the pleasant rush I've been feeling simply from our nonstop, easy conversation takes a turn toward something hotter ... and dangerous.

I shoot her a sideways glance, but she only smiles innocently. "I have to think so, remember. You're my beloved fiancé."

"Right," I say, hoping she can't tell that I'm rattled. Of course she was playing a role. And what the hell is wrong with me that I assumed she was marching straight into the forbidden zone?

*Cayden.* That's what's wrong with me. And damn the man for putting ideas into my head. Or, more accurately, for dragging to the forefront ideas that I'd been trying to suppress.

"Here," she says, and it takes me a second to realize that she's pointing at the turn.

"Are you sure? We're still about ten miles outside of Fredericksburg."

"I'm sure," she says. "*Turn.*"

I do, executing such a sharp turn that she leans toward me, her hand going to my thigh as she steadies herself. And I force myself not to think about how much more sense it would make for her to have steadied herself with the console between us.

She stays like that until I have us back in the proper lane. Then she slowly moves her hand to her lap. And, damn me, I not only regret the loss of contact, I mentally chastise myself for not pressing my hand on top of hers and holding her firmly in place.

After all, we're almost there. Maybe it's time to get into character.

I should point that out, I think. But when I speak, all I say is, "So where is this place, anyway?"

"It's called the Lavender Inn and Resort, and it's sort of behind the city." She has the map up on her phone and she uses two fingers too zoom in. "We're definitely going the right way. But it looks like we could have gone through Fredericksburg, too, then turned after the city. We'd sort of be backtracking, though. This way's faster."

I almost suggest that we take the long way so that we can scope out Fredericksburg's Main Street. That, of course, is my excuse. In reality, I'm enjoying the drive far too much to want it to end soon. That's selfish, though. This is her best friend's wedding, and I know she's looking forward to getting to the resort and seeing the bride.

After about fifteen minutes of driving past vineyards and fields of wildflowers, we arrive at the resort. From the street, we can see only the stone fence and iron gate opening onto a private drive. We follow it, and when we crest a small hill, we can see the entire resort spread out below us.

There's a pale blue Victorian mansion front and center, with a gravel parking area in front and beautiful flowerbeds. "That's the main house," Sam says. She's pulled a brochure out of her tote and is comparing the photos to the vista spread out before us. "That's where our room is. We're in the Luckenbach Suite."

"And see over there?" She points, and I see several smaller buildings. "The converted carriage house is the bridal suite. And the row of stables on the other side of the pool? Those have been converted into suites as well."

"And the other buildings?"

"Not sure. Probably conference rooms? And I think there's a gym and spa facilities. It's nice, don't you think?"

"Very. Thanks for handing me an unexpected, free vacation."

"Well, not really free. You have a job to do."

"Being your smitten fiancé? That's not a job. It's a perk."

I hadn't intended to say that, and I'm about to call back the words, but before I get the chance, she smiles. Then very softly says, "I'm really glad to hear that."

It's one of those moments when you're not really sure what to do next. When nothing seems quite right and even the passage of time feels surreal. Then someone behind me honks, the world crashes back into normalcy, and I realize I'm still stopped in the road at the top of the hill.

I wave an apology, then move slowly toward the main house, mindful of the ducks waddling toward us from a small pond on our right.

As I pull into the parking area, we can see three women talking on the wrap-around porch. "That's Cherry," Sam says, pointing to the curly-haired blonde in the middle.

I kill the engine. "You really didn't know that Thorne's her cousin?"

She shrugs. "Is that so hard to believe? I have no idea who your cousins are."

"But we're not dating."

"Right." She clears her throat as she glances back toward Cherry. "Good point. Although, you are smitten with me. As of right now," she adds, tossing me a casual smile.

"I am," I agree. "Which is why I will unload the luggage so you can go say hi to your friend."

"I have the best fake fiancé ever." She bends toward me, kisses my cheek, then slips out of the car so quickly I barely have time to register the way my cheek tingles from the lingering warmth.

Job perk, my ass. This is going to be torture.

But when I watch her laughing as she hugs her friend, I know that it's a torture I'll happily endure. Sam should enjoy her friend's special day, and if I weren't here as a buffer between her and the Thorne in her side, I know she'd be on edge.

I've pulled out her bag and am reaching for mine when I hear footsteps. I look up to see a guy in black jeans, a pristine white Henley with a Lavender Inn monogram, and a scruffy blond beard. He looks like an out-of-work model, and I assume he's just working here until Hollywood comes calling.

"I'll help with that," he says.

"Thanks. I check in through there?" I point to what I assume is the main entrance.

"Yup."

"Terrific. So if you can handle the bags, I'll meet you at reception." I take out my wallet and offer him a ten-spot.

He shakes his head, then starts laughing. "That's what I get for being helpful. I'm not the bellman. I saw you drive up with Sam." He extends his hand to me, all smiles and charm. "I'm Reg."

## CHAPTER FIVE

MY EYES DART TO SAM, who's shooting me a
*What The Fuck* look, which pretty much sums up
exactly how I feel.

"Sorry," Thorne says, obviously clueing in to our
nonverbal communication. "I didn't mean for us to get
off on the wrong foot."

"No, it's fine. I was just in the wrong mindset." I
point to the monogram. "The shirt."

"Oh, hell." His fingers trace the words. "I didn't
even think about that. My fault."

"No worries," I assure him.

"You'll have one, too, once you get to your room.
Anyway, great meeting you. I'll let you two get checked
in. Tell Sam I'll say hi to her later."

"Will do," I assure him, silently congratulating
his decision to postpone that greeting, especially

since Sam hasn't made the slightest move this direction.

He claps me on the shoulder, then heads off. The moment he disappears around the side of the building, Sam hurries to my side.

"I'm so sorry," she says, stooping to pick up her bag.

I stop her, reaching for the handle. "I got this. I told you."

She makes a face. "That was before. Now I want to get off the porch and into our room as soon as possible. And then I want you to tell me every single word he said."

I quash an absurd spurt of jealousy, then grab both suitcases over her protests and lead the way into the Inn. We've just reached the ramp onto the porch when a swarthy teen in the same Henley—this one with *Matt* embroidered over the logo—introduces himself as the guest liaison. He takes our names, and tells us that we're all checked in. He gives us the keys to the Luckenbach Suite, assures us a bellman will be right behind with the luggage, and leads us to our room.

It's easy enough to find. The house is three stories, with four suites on the main floor, along with a sitting area, kitchen and dining area. Two more suites are on the second floor, and the third is set up as a media room.

Since we're in one of the first floor suites, we only

hear rather than see Matt's description of the other floors. "I'm happy to give you the full tour," he tells us, but I assure him that we'll explore on our own. I want to check out our room. And I want to have some time to put on my game face.

Sam, I can tell, just wants to get someplace where we can talk.

Being an agreeable sort, Matt leads us into our suite, and as I jolt to a stunned stop, I hear Sam gasp. "Wow," she whispers, and Matt beams, as pleased as if he'd designed and decorated it himself.

The suite is huge, and we've stepped into a sitting room appointed with period furniture and drapes. Matt pulls the drapes aside, letting in more light and revealing a set of French doors, beyond which I can see a small garden.

"Your private entrance," Matt says. "There's a gate in the garden's left wall that opens onto the pool area. So you can come and go this way without going through the house."

We check out the fragrant garden, then peek at the sparkling pool, and I regret not bringing trunks. Then again, I could get equally behind a beer or margarita while sitting by the pool in shorts. Especially if that activity involves watching Sam.

When we go back inside, Matt shows us the tiny service area. "Just coffee and a small fridge for water, juice, wine. Whatever. But you have full access to the house kitchen, and of course we serve breakfast and dinner, along with a light lunch and snacks."

He shows us the master bathroom next, entering off the sitting area. It's equipped with a steam shower that features wall jets as well as a rain-style shower head. A huge clawfoot tub, that is more than adequate for two, serves as the focal point for the room. I wonder if we'll get to test it out, then immediately chastise myself for letting my mind go that direction.

We exit through the other door, this one leading directly into the master bedroom. Which, in fact, is the only bedroom. The bed is queen sized, surrounded by royal-style drapes, and made up with a lush spread and silk pillows in various shades of red. There are also two complimentary shirts, monogramed with the resort logo.

The whole room screams decadence and sensuality, and I decide right then that it's best not to look at Sam. As it is, it's going to be awkward enough sharing a queen bed. I'd been expecting a king. And a sofa bed. Or at least a couch.

But while the sitting room furniture is lovely, it's also period. Which means it really wasn't made for sleeping.

Which means we're sharing a bed.

I considered that both a perk ... and a potentially dangerous situation.

"Well," Matt says with his bright guest services smile, "I think that's everything. The resort is fully occupied by the wedding party and guests, so your group has the run of the place. There's an itinerary for the weekend on the desk in the sitting area. And I imagine your cases are already waiting in the hall. I'll roll them inside on my way out. And please, enjoy your stay."

I hand him the tip I'd tried to give to Reg, and Sam and I wait until we hear the door shut behind him. Then I turn to Sam and let out a low whistle. "I don't know about you, but I'm a little intimidated." I've been all over the world, but most of that travel was courtesy of the military. I'm not embarrassed to say I've never stayed in any place quite this luxurious.

Thankfully, Sam laughs. "No kidding, right?"

"We'll have to make a point to enjoy it."

She lifts her chin so that she's looking me straight in the eye. "I'm one hundred percent behind that plan."

There's not a damn thing suggestive about her words, but once again, they ricochet through me, an unexpected sensual assault.

She takes a step back, then moves into the living area. I follow, watching as she heads to her luggage. "I saw you guys talking," she says as she casually rolls the case toward the bedroom.

It's clear she's referring to Thorne, not Matt, and unwelcome pinpricks of jealousy poke at me. "I thought he worked here. The shirt."

She nods, as if acknowledging the reasonableness of my mistake. "So you didn't talk about anything else?"

"He said he'd tell you hi later. And I didn't get a devil vibe at all. Honestly, he seems like a nice enough guy." I get that she's upset at being tossed over for another woman, but maybe they simply weren't right for each other.

She crosses her arm and cocks her head. "I didn't realize you thought I was a shallow idiot."

*Okay.* That wasn't the response I was expecting. "Hello? What did I do?"

"Do you really think I'd go out with an obvious jerk just because he's easy on the eyes? Of course he seems nice. That's how devils suck you in."

I concede the point, wondering if I'll get any hints of Reg's devilish qualities over the course of the weekend. To be honest, I'd just as soon not see the guy again. But considering this entire performance is for his benefit, I know that won't happen.

"How's Cherry?" I ask, mostly to shift the subject away from The Ex.

"Nervous. Excited. But Peach and Daisy are keeping her calm, I think." She lifts her hard shell suitcase onto the bed and unzips it.

"Peach and Daisy?" I ask, sitting on the end of the bed and watching as she withdraws summery dresses, shorts, and—yes—lacy underwear and bras.

What I don't see her unpack is any sort of nightgown or pajamas. And, of course, that sets my imagination spiraling.

"They're her sisters," Sam says, her words having no connection whatsoever to the movie in my head.

"What? Who?"

"Peach and Daisy." She pauses on the way to the dresser, a tantalizing pile of panties in her hands. "You asked who the other girls with Cherry were."

"Right. Sorry. Mind wandering."

Her brows do a little dip and rise routine that I can't interpret, but then she continues as if there was nothing awkward about her lingerie or my inappropriate thoughts. "Don't get any of them started on the names. They've embraced them now, but as kids they did nothing but complain about their parents."

"Have you met the groom?"

"Not yet. I told you we're besties, but we moved apart after college. We still keep in touch and talk all the time, though. And for years we've been taking at least one vacation together." She frowns. "I guess that'll change now, won't it?"

"Jealous?"

"Of her getting married? Of course not. It's not like I'm ready to settle down. I mean, I still haven't figured out what I want to be when I grow up."

Considering I thought she was deeply entrenched in the world of computer games, that surprises me, but before I can ask, she continues.

"I guess I'm just bummed that he'll get Cherry's time now instead of me." She lifts her shoulder philosophically. "But I guess that's life."

"I guess it is. I felt the same way after Brody and Karen got together."

"Me, too."

"But in the long run it didn't really change our friendship."

"No, you guys are still incredibly close. And so are me and Bro, too." She sighs, then shakes her head. "I still can't believe Karen's gone. She was like a sister. And Brody—god, he was so damn broken. I didn't have a clue what to do for him."

"Me, either," I admit. "He's doing better."

"Lots," she says. "I think he's almost ready to start dating again. I hope he does. I think he's afraid he'll never find a love like that again, but I don't think that's true."

I lean forward, my elbow on my knee as I study her. "Don't you?"

"I think my brother's one of those people with a really big heart. He has room there for another love without shoving Karen out at all."

"That's nice," I say, genuinely moved by her words, and hoping that she's right. I've never spent much time thinking about settling down myself, but Brody seems incomplete without Karen, and the thought that another woman might make him whole again gives me hope.

"It is." She tugs out her toiletry bag, the last thing in her suitcase, then starts for the bathroom. "I want to be that in love someday," she says, her wistful voice drifting back to me. "But it has to be mutual. And I sometimes think that being Brody's sister is a bad thing. He made it look too easy."

She sounds far too melancholy, and I wonder if she's thinking about Reg and the way their relationship crumbled without warning.

I get up and cross to the open bathroom door. She's putting out bottles and tubes and brushes, a strand of dark hair falling over one eye. She lifts her head and watches my reflection, but says nothing.

"I think we're starting to bring down the mood," I say gently. "And it's way too pretty a day to do that. Why don't I unpack, and then we can go explore?"

She hesitates only a second, then nods. "That sounds like a great plan."

While I put my things away, she reads through the weekend itinerary. "So we officially start at seven tonight, and after that it's pretty much non-stop activities until the sunset ceremony on Sunday."

"That gives us about four free hours. It's been years since I've been to Fredericksburg. I say we check out the town. You?"

"A town famous for its wineries. Yeah, I'm in. And believe it or not, I've never been here before. My life before Seattle was pretty Dallas-centric."

Since neither of us is sure where to start, we head off to the guest services desk.

Reg is at the counter looking at a brochure, and as he turns to us, Samantha molds herself to my side. I slide into my appointed role, possibly too eagerly, and hook an arm around her waist.

"Samantha, you look incredible as always."

"Reg."

An awkward silence lingers, thankfully broken by the woman manning the desk, who asks how she can help us.

I step closer to the desk, shifting my connection with Sam until we're simply holding hands. Then I explain that we're hoping to explore the town and check out a few local wines.

"Happy to help," she assures me, then pulls out a map and a red pen. "The local wineries are scattered around the area," she tells us, "but many of them have tasting rooms in town or a presence in the pubs or restaurants."

"I took a stroll this morning after we unpacked," Reg says. "Lovely town."

"How smart of you to unpack," I hear Sam say from behind me. I frown, not sure what she means, then have to force myself not to stiffen in surprise when she presses against my back and slides her arms around my waist. I feel her breasts, soft against me, and the pressure of her body against my ass.

"Ah, yes," I say in response to the woman's suggestion that she highlight the places she thinks we'd most enjoy. "That would be very helpful."

"Leo and I planned to unpack. But we got sidetracked." She giggles—a very unSam-like sounds—and I about lose it when her body rises up, rubbing cat-like against mine, and her tongue traces the back of my ear, sending coils of shimmering heat spiraling through me. "We're always getting sidetracked," she murmurs, her voice suggesting that we're about to be sidetracked right now.

"That's your fault, sweetheart," I say in the kind of voice I've only used in a bedroom. I tug her around, so that she's beside me, our arms around each other. "You are far too distracting."

As Sam seems to melt against me, I return the woman's charmed smile—I imagine she sees a lot of affectionate couples—then turn to Reg.

I deliberately shift my expression from dreamy to casually polite. "Sorry. Our friends always give us shit for too much PDA. But we just can't help it."

A muscle in his cheek twitches. "Well, you're still in that new phase. Totally understandable. I'm sure you'll be able to keep your hands to yourselves soon enough."

I flash a thin smile. Maybe he is the devil after all. He's definitely a prick. "I wouldn't say we're new, would you, baby?" It's a risk, because I have absolutely no idea how long ago they broke up. But since he's engaged now, I figure it's worth a shot.

"Not new at all." Her eyes lock on mine, and right then I really could drown in those chocolate depths. "Amazing that almost four months can feel like yesterday."

"Four—" Reg stops himself and spreads his hands, his handsome face marred by a plastic smile. And that's when I know how long they've been apart. Right at four months.

"That's great," he says flatly. "And I hope she

didn't bore you too much talking about me. We had an amicable split, but these things still hurt."

"Oh." I intentionally furrow my brow. "That's really decent of you to worry about her—and us. But it's all good. She didn't even mention your name until Cherry invited us to the wedding. And I promise," I add in what I hope sounds like a manly, conspiratorial voice, "I'm working very hard to make sure she doesn't have the time or the inclination to think about any man who came before me."

I can practically feel Samantha vibrating with amusement as Reg's face turns an interesting shade of puce.

"Well," he finally says, "I'm glad you two found each other."

"Yeah," I say, brushing my thumb over her lips as she makes a show of sighing happily. "So are we."

## CHAPTER SIX

"I'M STILL SEEING HIS FACE," Sam says, hooking her arm through mine as we move on to our third tasting room. Although, honestly, *stumble* might be a better description.

Reg has not, thankfully, been the only topic of conversation during our exploration of the charming Main Street area. On the contrary, we've covered a variety of Fredericksburg-inspired topics, including wine, wildflowers, folk art, women's clothing, leather goods, country music, architecture, and even naval aircraft carriers thanks to the Pacific War Museum.

Now, we're heading to a local bar that we've heard distills its own whiskey. Possibly not the best plan on top of two wine-tastings of three flights each, but the goal is to experience the town in the hours we have before the festivities kick in.

"Four months," she continues, then giggles when I say that it seems like only yesterday.

This whole shift back to Thorne came about when the sommelier at our last stop asked how long we'd been dating. Sam's eyes went wide, but I have to hand it to myself, because I pulled that story right back out of the vault where I'd dropped it. And it was worth it when I saw Samantha's smile.

"Thanks," she'd said as we worked our way through the flights.

"For what?"

"For staying in character even though we're not around anybody who matters."

"You matter." The words had just slipped out, true but probably not prudent. Not the way I think I meant them. And that was a way I *couldn't* think about. Not then. Because more and more, Samantha Watson was getting under my skin. And I still wasn't sure what to do about that.

"I just mean your mission," I said, backtracking. "I'm all in, and that means I'm staying in character twenty-four/seven."

"All right," she'd said, her voice a little reedy from alcohol. "I shall hold you to that."

She'd nodded, as if we'd just sealed some deal, but before I could press her on it, she shifted the conversation to Cherry and asked if we should get her some sort of hostess gift while we were out and about. "I brought a wedding present, but I've never been to a destination wedding before."

Since that wasn't really my department, I listened —enchanted—while she worked it out for herself, finally deciding to get her a best friend gift that was entirely separate from the wedding goings-on.

That's part of what we're doing now. Searching out a fun and funky—Sam's words—gift as we make our way to the whiskey bar.

"Whoa, whoa," I say, when I see the sign for The Oak Room, the bar we've been aiming for. She's moved ahead, so I tug her back, and she does a dance style twirl into my arms. Laughing, I dip her, to the delight of a passing couple who pauses long enough to applaud.

"We are so wasted," she whispers to me, after we've bowed to our audience and are heading inside.

"Nope," I correct. "This is all part of the plan. We need to be comfortable together."

She tugs me out of the doorway, then hooks her arms around my neck. Her body is warm, and not just from the lovely spring weather. And her lips—glossed with a strawberry balm she bought in a cute shop on the last block—glisten with invitation.

"I've been comfortable around you my whole life, Leonardo Vincent Palmero. Is that really news to you?"

Her voice is so soft I can almost tell myself that I'm imagining the words. But I know I'm not, and my breath catches in my throat as I gamely try to fight temptation. Because at the moment, there is nothing I want more in the world than to taste her.

"Table for two?"

The bright, cheerful voice pulls me back to reality. Sam, too, I realize, when she takes a step back, her face flushing pink. "No," she whispers. "No, actually we can't stay. We, um, just came in to buy a bottle of whiskey. We heard it's really good, and, um, well, it's a present."

"No problem at all," the clueless hostess says. "We do a great gin, too, and you get a discount if you buy two."

"Sure. Great. Perfect."

"Fab! I'll be right back. You can meet me at the register."

As the girl heads to the back, I tilt my head in question, but Sam only shrugs. "It's getting late, and I should shower before tonight's cocktail party. And, you know. Do we really need more drinks when tonight is all about toasting the couple?"

I nod my agreement, even though what I want to say is that hell yes we need more drinks, because I'm

not allowed to have this woman, and that means I want
to be numb. But all I say is, "Right. Of course.
Honestly, I may take a walk while you clean up. Clear
the alcohol haze out of my head."

"Sure. Great idea."

It *was* a great idea, because as much as drinking
myself to numbness sounded like one hell of a plan, it
was also doomed to failure. Drinking lowers
inhibitions, and right now I needed to keep a tight hold
on my self-control. Not an easy task considering it was
Sam I wanted to hold onto.

Honestly, what the hell was I thinking? Not about
Brody, that was for damn sure. More than that, as
much as Sam tempts me—and she tempts me a lot—I
don't want a random hook-up with someone important
to me.

Hell, I don't want a hook-up at all. Not with her,
not with anybody. This isn't a dry spell that I'm going
through—I know that. I just haven't let myself think
about it. But the bouncing from bed to bed with no real
connection isn't just getting old, it's gotten boring.
Meaningless.

But there's nothing boring or meaningless about
Samantha.

And she deserves a hell of a lot more than what
little I have to offer.

Which means that what's supposed to be a light

and easy weekend of role-playing with the little girl I used to tease is turning out to be not so easy after all.

Because damned if I don't want her.

And *that* is exactly what I can't have.

## CHAPTER SEVEN

THE RESORT IS HUGE, but I intend to walk every square inch of it over the next sixty minutes. I've got two water bottles with me, and I take long swallows from each, hoping the liquid and the motion will wash the alcohol right out of my system—not to mention the lingering effects that Samantha's left on my now all-too-tense body.

I see Reg as I set out. He's in one of the converted stables, and the entrance to his unit faces the pool. His door is clearly visible from our back gate, which is where he's standing as I leave Samantha to enjoy her shower in peace. Although to be honest, my motives for leaving weren't entirely altruistic. The idea of being alone in the room while she's naked and soapy wasn't doing my tightly-strung body any favors.

I nod to Reg, and for an uncomfortable moment I

think he's going to try to catch up with me. But I adjust my ear buds, pretend I haven't noticed him signaling me to hold up, and keep on walking. By the time I glance back, he's nowhere to be seen.

I feel no guilt. After all, I don't like the guy. More important, my role here is to be Samantha's devoted arm candy. And that's a role best played at her side.

I quickly banish thoughts of Reg from my mind, but despite my good intentions, Sam lingers in my head for the entirety of my walk. I think about her as I wave to Cherry, wondering how their friendship will change and if Samantha will ever marry. The guy would be a lucky bastard, that's for sure, and I tell myself that the tight knot in my stomach isn't jealousy. Not by a long shot.

I think about her on the grassy lawn with the long stone table and fairy lights strung in the trees. The sun hasn't set yet, but it'll be twilight when the cocktail party starts, and the place will look magical. Samantha, I think, deserves all the magic she can get.

I think about her as I once again pass the pool, imagining her silky body cutting through the water, her long hair hanging in wet strands as she steps out, her nipples hard beneath a thin, white bikini.

And, damn me, I think about her as I step through the gate back into our private garden. She'll be out of the shower by now, and I'd caught a glimpse of a flirty red cocktail dress as she'd unpacked. I hope she's wearing it tonight. It will bring out the hints of red in her dark brown hair.

The drapes are drawn, so I try the door quietly in case she's taking a nap. It's unlocked, and I gently pull it open, then ease past the curtain.

The sitting area is empty, so I head toward the bedroom, only to stop dead in my tracks the moment I hit the threshold.

She's standing right there in front of a chest of drawers, her back to me, wearing nothing but a towel. There's a mirror mounted above the chest, but I already know that the angle of that wall is such that it doesn't reflect the doorway.

I should cough. Speak. Do something. But I don't. I simply stand there as she opens the top drawer, pulls out something red and flimsy that I assume is a pair of panties, then reaches between her breasts, loosens the towel, and lets it drop to the floor.

I suck in a breath, stunned out of my stupor by my overwhelming desire to touch her. Her body's not perfect by traditional standards. *Sports Illustrated* won't be coming to call. But by God, I've never seen anyone lovelier. Her legs have already enchanted me, but now her hips claim me, too. They're narrow, but well defined by her small waist, just the right size to get my hands around. And her ass is more rounded and firm than it seems when she's wearing denim. I can imagine my hands cupping her rear as I pull her close to me, naked and ready and craving me.

I almost moan, then force the sound to stay in my throat, not wanting her to know I'm there. Wanting another few seconds of this forbidden moment.

Then I realize she's not moving at all. The hand with the red silk is still extended. Her shoulders haven't shifted. She's not even breathing.

*She knows I'm behind her.*

A wave of self-loathing washes over me. I have no right to invade her privacy like this. I owe her more than an apology, but damned if I can find the words.

I'm searching for something to say when she slowly turns her head, and I hold my breath, expecting her to bend for the towel. To cover herself, then lay into me, and I'm prepared to do nothing but weather the blows.

But she doesn't bend. And it's not just her head that she turns toward me. She shifts her entire body, her arms at her sides so that no part of her is covered. Her breasts are firm, her nipples erect. The muscles in her belly quiver, the only hint that she's the slightest bit nervous, and her slightly spread legs put her lovely waxed pussy on display. I suck in air, and damned if I can't look away. She's incredible. She's everything, and I realize my mouth is open, but there aren't any words. I have no idea what to say, and I'm aroused and ashamed and astounded all at the same time.

"Hey," she says, the heat in her voice giving me all the permission I thought that I lacked. She takes a step toward me, then another and another, until she's right in front of me, entirely bare and close enough to touch.

I want to—so help me, I do—but despite an obvious invitation, I can't move a muscle.

"How was your walk?"

"Fine." My voice is a croak.

"So was my shower. I missed you."

"Sam..."

She comes closer, and I catch the scent of strawberries in the freshness of her damp hair. "It's okay, you know."

But it's not. I hear Brody's voice in my head. Hell, I hear my own. I'm tired of hook-ups. Tired of sex for sex's sake. And I absolutely do not want to fuck up half a lifetime of friendship between me and Brody or between me and Sam.

"It's not," I say. "I'm sorry. You're so damn tempting. But I can't. I need—I just can't."

I turn and walk back to the curtain, still covering the French doors. I want to look back, to see if I've leveled her. I hope I haven't. Surely a woman with the balls to do what she just did will survive one freaked out man.

But I can't even turn back. Because the truth is, I want what she's offering, and I'm afraid if I look, I'll take it. But that's something I just can't do.

————

I wander without purpose, once again thinking about Cayden's prophetic words—*blue balls*.

Yup. He definitely got that right.

My phone chirps, and I yank it out of my pocket hoping it's Sam, only to see that it's the only other person in my thoughts at the moment—Cayden.

"You just can't live without me," I say.

"How's it going?"

"Not bad. The resort's beautiful."

"And the girl?"

"She's beautiful, too."

"I meant has she gotten you in bed yet?"

*Almost, and damn did I want to.*

"You're an ass," I tell him. "You know that, right?"

"Just giving you shit. And one more piece of advice."

"Great."

"All I'm saying is that you need to look at what's in front of you, not some screen that Brody's thrown up to block the view."

"Cayden—"

"I'm serious, man. Connor just about lost Kerrie because he was too stubborn, and I almost didn't see Gracie because I was so blinded by what happened before. Sam's a grown woman, not an appendage of Brody. That's all I'm saying."

"I hear you. Is that really why you called? Because that seems a little too touchy-feely, even for you."

"Hey, I'm a born again romantic. But, no. Actually, I need to ask you about the Mendez workup. Kerrie says you updated the file, but I don't see a hard copy or an electronic version."

"Shit," I say, as I relax into the rhythm of work, a much safer mindset even if there's a minor crisis. "Maybe it's stuck on my hard drive. We really need to get a dedicated IT person, because this has happened more than once."

I continue my gripe about the dysfunctional automatic file sharing system until he gets to my office, and I walk him through how to access my files. We go over a few key points about the workup, then wrap it up.

"Great. Thanks. Sorry to bug you during your vacation."

"No sweat. And Cayden—"

"Yeah?"

I hesitate, then shake my head. "Nothing. I'll call

you when I'm back in town. You can come drink a beer and watch me unpack."

"You sure know how to show a fellow a good time."

He ends the call, and I draw a deep breath as I think about Brody. I should call him. Especially since I'm damn sure that hearing his voice will chill my lustful thoughts about his sister.

I'm still holding my phone, and now I pull up Brody in my contacts. I start to hit the button to dial, but my finger can't quite manage it. And then, with a sharp, heartfelt curse, I shove the damn thing back into my pocket and head back to the suite so that I can change for cocktails.

# CHAPTER EIGHT

IF I DIDN'T HAVE to talk to Reg, the cocktail party would be just about perfect. The drinks range from wine to fancy cocktails to straight up whiskey. The ambiance is incredible. The bride and groom are charming and happy. And there's not even a hint of awkwardness between Sam and me.

On the contrary, she's all smiles as she brings me a fresh Scotch and water, then offers to track down a slice of Snickers cheesecake, a featured treat on the dessert cart that she promises is entirely coincidental.

"Stay," I urge when I see Reg heading in my direction, willing to sacrifice even a Snickers fix in order to not see him alone. "We're supposed to be so sappy he goes into sugar shock."

"Nope. I just need him to know what an amazing guy I landed. So amaze him while I go find you cheesecake." She rises up to kiss my cheek, then disappears into the throng as I stand still, wondering why she didn't issue me a cigarette and blindfold, too.

My initial impression of Reg as a thoughtful guy has long since faded. He struck the first nail when we were at the concierge desk, and every time we've crossed paths—which has been far too many times this evening—his coffin is sealed tighter and tighter.

"Busy day," he says, raising his own drink to me. "I haven't yet gotten the vice-president position, but everyone is so sure that it'll be mine officially next week that I'm fielding all the VP calls."

"You must be very busy."

"It's a non-stop kind of life that really only suits a certain personality type. Someone who can tackle different problems every day. Who can manage people as well as business. Who can look five steps into the future and see what's coming."

"Mmm," I say, because what else is there?

"And the double-dealing. You can't imagine the extent of corporate espionage in this industry. Considering our business is games, it's ridiculously cutthroat. Hell, there are probably spies here at the resort trying to find out about our upcoming roll-out or get a glimpse of next quarter's financials."

"I think it's the underlying technology that's driving

the espionage. Not the actual games." Shouldn't a guy in the industry understand that better than a security specialist who only plays the things on occasion?

He waves my words aside. "I'm sure this is all dull to you. Certainly not the kind of environment you would thrive in. Or even understand. Though I suppose actors do need some surface knowledge of the careers their characters are in."

"Mmm." Though actor wasn't my first choice—I suggested test pilot—Sam had reasonably pointed out that I could fake being an actor much easier than a pilot. Especially since Reg's father owned a single engine Cessna.

Now, I consider making up a production company that's getting bought out by Disney and will turn me into a multimillionaire overnight, but I decide against it. I'm not an actor, but he is a prick. So we might as well just stick with the status quo.

And with any luck, Sam will be back soon.

"I'm lucky, really. Even with a talent like mine, it's not always recognized. Fortunately, Lisa's father saw that in me. I have him to thank for my upcoming promotion. Well, him and some remarkable assets I'm bringing to the table."

"Lisa?" I ask, pretending I have no idea who he's talking about.

"My fiancée," he says. "Lisa Bronwyn. We fell head-over-heels for each other."

"Is she here?"

He shakes his head. "Unfortunately, she had to cancel at the last minute. But since Cherry's my cousin, I wanted to be here for her."

"Kind of you," I say, then smile more broadly than is usually required of cheesecake when Sam returns.

"None for me?" Reg asks. His voice is teasing, but Sam's reply is harsh.

"I think you've gotten everything you'll ever get from me." She turns to me. "Honey, you haven't had the chance to talk much with Cherry. Let's go find her."

In fact, she introduced me to Cherry when we first got to the party, and we'd had a long, pleasant conversation after which I told Sam that I thought the bride to be absolutely worthy of Sam's friendship.

"Where are we really going?" I ask.

"Away from Reg. I figured that was enough."

"I could kiss you right now," I tell her, in response to which she tilts her head up.

"Do," she says. "He's watching."

Unlike earlier, I don't hesitate. Earlier was bonus content. This is the actual show, and I take her into my arms, then use my finger to lift her chin as I close my mouth over hers. I'm planning on sensual and romantic. A solid show-kiss for a mixed audience.

But things don't always go the way they're planned. Her lips part, her mouth opening wide to me, and I don't even hesitate. I claim it hungrily, reveling in the way our tongues war and our teeth clash as she clutches the back of my head and pulls me tighter against her. This is more than a kiss, it's a full-on sensual assault, and I feel the effects of it burning through me, heating my blood, firing my senses.

My head spins, and I don't want this to end, and when we break apart, she takes my hand. "We need to go to the room now."

"Why?" My defenses are down, but despite that kiss, my pre-Brody position hasn't changed.

"Because they'll all think that we're going off to fuck—Reg among them. And that's what we want them to think."

"Right." I draw in a breath, feeling a bit cheated that they'll think it even though we aren't doing it.

"It's still an option," she says a few minutes later once we're inside the suite.

We've walked halfway across the resort, but I still know what she's talking about. Primarily because that's all I've been thinking about. "Samantha..."

Her eyes narrow, then she cocks her head toward the bedroom. "Follow me."

"Sam, you know we're not..."

"A game," she says. "We're just going to play a game."

She climbs onto the bed, gathering her skirt around her bent legs. Then she pats the mattress in front of her.

I hesitate, but I've had a few drinks and a nice little buzz, and why wouldn't I want to play a game with this woman?

So, yeah. I join her. Albeit with a tiny bit of trepidation.

"What are we playing?" I ask.

"Truth or Dare. Or Never Have I Ever." Her mouth curves in a magnanimous smile. "Your choice."

"You do realize we're not in school anymore."

"Yes, thank you, I know. But I also know what I want."

"And what's that?"

"Isn't it obvious? I want to play this game with you. Why? Are you too shy?"

"Maybe I'm not sure I want all my secrets revealed."

"No problem," she says cheerily. "Truth or Dare it is. Then you never have to tell me anything—you can always choose a dare if you want." She points toward the sitting room. "We'll keep the whiskey, by the way, and I'll take Cherry the gin when I meet the girls at the spa in the morning."

She waves her hand again. "Well, go on. The bottle's on the desk and there are glasses in the serving area."

I should protest, but I don't. Why? Because even though I should, I want to play. And I hope she chooses truth most of the time, because I want to hear her secrets. And because if she takes the dare option, I'm really not sure what I'll make her do.

I bring the glasses and the bottle, but forego the ice as I pour us each a shot. "We drink on the questions or the dares," she says, and although I'm quite sure those aren't the formal rules, I nod in agreement.

She says I can start, and when I pose the question, she chooses truth.

"Who was the last person you slept with?"

"Reg," she says. "But tonight I'll sleep with you."

"*Beside* me," I correct.

She lifts a shoulder. "We'll see. Truth or dare."

"Dare."

She takes a sip as she ponders, and even though we're only drinking on questions, I don't stop her. For that matter, I take one myself. Spirit of the game and all.

"All right," she says. "Take off your shirt."

I figure I've gotten off easy. I'm wearing jeans and a

gray linen button down, and as soon as I've taken it off, I toss it off the side of the bed.

Her teeth drag over her lower lip as her eyes explore me. "Nice," she says, and that simple word pleases me more than it should. Then her brows arch in confusion, and she points to a spot a few inches down from my shoulder.

"Shrapnel," I say before she can ask. "Caught it in Afghanistan. And we're not talking about my time in the military. This game isn't supposed to be serious."

"Oh, it's serious," she counters. "But I'm fine with that rule." She finishes her whiskey and holds out the glass for more. "Your turn to ask," she says as I pour.

I do, and this time she chooses dare. And for a moment—one moment for which I should be desperately ashamed—I consider the possibility of daring her to suck my cock.

I shove the thought away, though. Because we are not going there.

Still ... even if I'm not going to fuck her, that doesn't mean I can't enjoy the view. "Take off your dress."

Without any protest, she unzips the back and pulls the whole thing over her head. Then she tosses it on top of my shirt.

Now she's sitting about two feet away from me in tiny panties and a strapless bra. I've seen her in less—

like absolutely nothing— but damn me, I'm harder now than I was this afternoon.

I slam back the rest of my drink and try to find some sort of equilibrium.

"My turn," she says. "Which is it?"

"You know."

"Fine. Another dare." Her eyes dip. "Take off your jeans."

*Shit.* I really should have seen that coming. "No can do," I say. "You'd be getting a disproportionate response."

"In English?"

"I'm commando."

"Bullshit."

"I'm serious." I realized when I was getting dressed that I forgot to pack underwear. I shrug. "It's no big deal. Except during truth or dare."

"I still think you're bullshitting me." As she says it, she scoots to my side.

"What the hell?" I ask as she tugs on my waistband, then slides her hand inside. "Christ Sam." My voice doesn't sound like my own, but I wasn't prepared for her warm palm against my stiffening cock.

"You're turned on," she says softly. "Me, too." She eases her hand out of my jeans, then resettles on the mattress across from me. Only this time, her legs aren't primly together and tucked behind her. Now she's in a lotus position, giving me a full view of her obviously wet panties. "Okay," she says, "truth or dare."

My heart is pounding. And, yeah, my resolve is fading. "It's your turn to choose."

She doesn't answer, but her eyes never leave mine as she slowly slides her fingers inside the band of her panties. "Stroke your cock."

"Jesus, Sam ... we said weren't going to do this."

"It's just a game." Her voice is low, heavy with sensual possibilities, and I can see her nipples harden under the thin satin of the bra. "You didn't make any promises to Brody about not playing games."

"Then let's play it," I say, my voice cracking with lust. "And it's your turn to choose."

She sighs in defeat, but her fingers linger where they are. "Truth," she says.

"Favorite sexual position?" Wonder why *that* was the first thought to come into my head.

"Yet to be determined. Want to help me figure it out?"

"Sam. Don't."

"Fine. Truth okay?"

I sigh. "Sure. Fine."

"What exactly did you promise my brother?"

I think about it, trying to replay the conversation. "That I wouldn't make a pass."

"Good info. I think we can work with that."

I shake my head. "No. There was subtext. That I wasn't going to fuck his sister."

"Not fuck," she clarifies. "He's afraid you'll seduce me. But that's not what's happening here, is it?"

No, I think. It's definitely not. But all I say is, "Sam..."

"Play the game."

"It's late, and you can barely keep your eyes open." It's true. She's finished her second whiskey, and she's definitely starting to fade.

"Just play the damn game."

"Fine. Dare."

"Watch." The fingers that had barely dipped into her underwater now ease lower to her clit. I can't see everything, but just knowing what she's doing under that thin scrap of material...

"God, Sam." She's driving me crazy. "You can't—"

"This is the dare. I'm daring you to watch. No touching me. No touching yourself. Just keep your eyes on me. Do you think you can?"

As she speaks, she tugs off the panties, then unfastens the bra. She's completely naked now, her skin practically glowing from arousal.

"I like you watching me," she says as she plays with her clit. Her eyes meet mine. "Do you like it, too?"

"It's dare," I say. "Not truth."

She closes her eyes and lifts her hips as she thrusts

two fingers deep inside. "Just tell me. Please, Leo. I want to hear you say it."

"Yes," I admit, so turned on now it's all I can do not to toss my promise away and fuck her right then. "I'm hard as a rock, and you're killing me. Truth or dare."

"Dare."

The word hangs in the air.

I draw a breath, knowing I'm about to cross a line. But that's okay, because it's the only line I intend to cross.

"Leo?" Her voice is soft. "Tell me. What's my dare?"

"Come for me," I whisper. "I dare you to come while I'm watching."

A smile dances on her lips, and I watch, mesmerized, as she fingers herself, her hips shifting and her body trembling as she comes closer and closer.

My cock's hard as steel, but I have no desire to jack off. I'm mesmerized by her sounds. By the way her muscles tighten and release. The rhythm of her hips.

And just when I think that I could watch her all night, she cries out, then arches up as she gasps for air, her fingers tightening in the mussed bedcover.

When her body finally stops trembling, she falls back against the pillows, then reaches for the decorative blanket that's folded at the foot of the bed. I put it over her, and she tugs it up around her shoulders as she smiles innocently at me.

"Night, Leo," she says, then rolls onto her side, the blanket hugging her bare body as she drifts off into a sex and whiskey induced sleep.

## CHAPTER NINE

WHEN I WAKE UP, Sam's side of the bed is empty, and the inside of the suite is both quiet and pitch black.

I sit bolt upright, then I click on the bedside lamp, terrified that she regretted putting on that surprising, amazing, seriously fucking hot show for me.

I check my phone and see that it's already past eleven. My imagination goes into overdrive, seeing her in a ride share, halfway to Austin by now. Or at the very least, sharing Cherry's room, since the bride and groom are in separate suites until after the ceremony.

But before I have time to either call her cell phone or conjure anymore nightmare scenarios, I find a note written in lipstick on the bathroom mirror.

*I hope you enjoyed the show.*
*I did.*

I still don't know where she's gone, but at least my heart has stopped pounding. Then I remember the itinerary and see that the women started their spa day at eight. The men are scheduled to start playing poker at one, following something the schedule calls a Bloody Mary Brunch.

I consider staying in. Sleeping. Berating myself for going so far with Sam yesterday despite knowing I shouldn't. Then berating myself even more because I enjoyed it so damn much. Maybe calling Brody and begging for forgiveness.

*Maybe taking a shower and jacking off to the memory of last night...*

Honestly, that's the most tempting option.

And the truth is, Sam's right. I haven't broken my word to Brody. Not literally, anyway.

I didn't fuck her, and I didn't seduce her.

Quite the opposite.

But damned if I don't want to.

I run my fingers through my hair, realizing I've made my decision about the day—and I'm going to get Bachelor Party-style sloshed on Bloody Marys, then lose enough at poker to appease what guilt I haven't yet justified.

First, though, I'm going to take a cold shower.

———

By the time the Saturday evening cocktail hour rolls around, I'm up just over two hundred dollars, all of which I donate to the bride and groom's honeymoon fund. From what Reg told me during breaks in the game, they wanted to do two weeks in Europe, but couldn't afford more than one, something I would never have guessed in light of this luxurious and undoubtedly expensive weekend.

But Reg anticipated that comment and explained that the resort's owner is Cherry's godfather, and the entire weekend is his present to her. Fabulous, but not the honeymoon. So now, family and friends are secretly building a fund that the couple can either spend on the trip or use to seed their savings.

Not that I was actively tugging information from Reg. On the contrary, I tried to escape him at every conversational break. But like a determined leech, he spent much of the afternoon at my side, primarily so he could interrogate me about Sam. If she ever mentioned him. If she told me about their time working together. If she seemed to harbor any bad feelings.

Totally surreal, and I wasn't sure if he was just feeling guilty for tossing her over for Lisa, or if Lisa's going to be out of the picture once he gets his promotion, and he'll set his sights back on Sam.

I told him that she'd barely spoken his name. I figured that ought to cool any lingering interest. Because I really can't stomach the thought of her back with this guy.

For that matter, I can't stand to think about her with any guy. Any guy other than me, that is.

I glance around, but only see a few women in the cocktail area, and Sam's not among them. I grab a glass of red wine from one of the linen covered tables and consider going to our room, where she's undoubtedly changing. Since that plan has a potentially dangerous outcome, I force myself to stay firmly in place.

Five minutes later, I'm rewarded when I see her and Cherry walking across the lawn, their faces alight as they laugh together. I draw a deep breath, mesmerized by this woman who is no longer the gangly, shy girl I used to know. Now, she's a woman I crave.

And a woman whose heart I would never risk breaking.

I know the moment she sees me. Her smile widens so bright it warms me even from this distance. She says something to Cherry, then hurries ahead, coming to a stop in front of me.

"You're sexy when you're sleeping," she says with an impish grin. "I almost skipped the spa just to stay in and watch you."

"I would have liked that," I admit as we walk toward one of the wooden benches. "But Sam, whatever happened last night, you know we can't—"

"Oh, but we can."

*Hell yeah we can.* But we shouldn't. And I don't like this feeling of walking on shifting ground. "Truth or dare?"

I hadn't intended to ask the question, and from her expression, Sam's as surprised by it as I am.

"What?"

"Truth or dare," I repeat, this time more firmly, because I know what I want now. "We'll go with truth. Why did you want me to come this weekend? Was it really to make Reg jealous? Because we've been behind closed doors more than we've been in his face."

She takes a seat. "Are you mad at me?"

"No—no, I'm not. I'm just—confused? I don't even know."

She watches me as I pace, then says softly, "So here's the thing. I don't give a fuck about Reg. Not that way. We didn't even date for that long."

I pause in front of her. "Then, why?"

"Leo, please, I—"

"Why?" I repeat.

She nods, then draws in one breath, then another. Then she polishes off her wine. "I'm going to need another of these."

TEMPTING LITTLE TEASE   95

"After."

"It's just that I've never—I can't believe I'm telling you this, but what happens in Fredericksburg stays in Fredericksburg, right?"

I think about all we've done as I sit down on the bench beside her. "Damn right."

"Okay. I'm just going to spit it out." She runs a finger over the top of her wineglass, her eyes focused on the movement and not on me. "I've had a crush on you forever. Just being around you when I was a kid. I felt so alive. You were the first—"

"What?" I ask when she cuts herself off sharply.

"Never mind."

"Well, now I really am intrigued. Tell me."

She squirms a bit, but finally mutters, "My very first, you know. When I was a teen and ... all that..."

I know where she's going, and it's sweet, but I also can't hide my amusement that the bold woman from last night is barely able to say these words without spontaneously combusting from a massive blush.

"Are you talking about what you did last night? What you dared me to watch? And you really can't say the words?"

Her eyes flash as she glances over at me. "Fine. The first time I masturbated to orgasm I was thinking about you. Better?"

I knew it, but hearing it's different. And, damn me, her confession turns me on.

"I've wanted you forever," she continues, obviously emboldened by her confession. "You've been a fantasy I've held up in other relationships. So I needed to make it real."

"Sam..."

She holds up a hand, as if anticipating my words. "I know you're not looking for a relationship. Neither am I. Really and truly. But I need to get past you. And, honestly, I want the fantasy made real."

She slides her hand to my crotch and rests her palm over the bulge of my erection. "And you can't deny that you want me, too. Maybe you didn't back when I first wanted you, but you want me now."

I don't—*can't*—deny it.

She presses harder. "Please." There's desperation in her voice. "Take me to bed, Leo. Wear me out. No strings, I swear. Just one wild, crazy, incredibly hot weekend. I want the real man. Then maybe I can let go of the fantasies and just move on."

"Sam, I—"

"Don't say it."

"What?"

"You were probably going to tell me that I shouldn't have said any of that—and you're probably right. But I've been drinking mimosas all day. And as we've already established, I have no inhibitions when I'm drunk around you."

I keep my voice low and gentle. "I wasn't going to say that."

"Then you were going to say that we can't do anything because of the shadow of big brother hanging over us. Well, guess what? This isn't 1984, and what my brother doesn't know won't hurt him."

"I wasn't going to say that either."

"Oh." She frowns. "Then—"

"I was going to say that I'm not sure if I'm flattered to be the object of your fantasies, or insulted that you think the real man doesn't live up to the dream lover."

For a moment she just stares at me. Then, very softly, she says, "But you aren't saying no."

"There have to be rules," I begin, as she nods eagerly. "If I'm going to break my best friend's trust—and you know that eventually he'll find out and give me grief no matter how careful we are—then I want to really deserve the punishment. Like seriously."

I see her throat move as she swallows, but her eyes dance with undisguised anticipation. "What does that mean?"

"Like you said. What happens in Fredericksburg stays in Fredericksburg. But it's my turn to call the shots, baby. I promise, you'll enjoy it."

She nods eagerly. "But nothing where we could get

caught. I'd die if something happened at Cherry's wedding to embarrass her or her family."

"Fair enough."

Her eyes widen just a bit. "We're really going to do this?"

The simple fact that she wants me so much is almost enough to make me come right then. "The sooner the better," I say, standing and holding out a hand to help her up. In the distance, I notice the other guests lining up at a buffet table. "Unless you want dessert?"

Her eyes dip to my crotch. "Actually, yes. But if it's all the same to you, I'll have it in our room."

## CHAPTER TEN

GETTING ALL the way to our room is an exercise in
self-control, because damned if I don't want to pull her
into every hidden corner we pass. Anyplace will do.
All I want is to have her right now, this very second. All
I want is to lose myself inside this woman who's been
driving me crazy since the moment I walked into her
house a few days ago.

Has it really only been days? It feels like I've
wanted her forever. Known her forever. And hell, I
*have* known her forever. Have I wanted her all along,
too, and just been too much of a damned idiot to
realize it?

I don't know, and I don't care. All that matters
is now.

All that matters is her.

"What are you thinking?" Her whispered words

are soft and a little raspy, as if she's struggling for control. I get it. So am I.

"About you. About how I'm not sure I can wait to have you."

"Leo..."

I have never in my life heard a woman speak my name with so much need, and the obvious depth of her desire sends waves of pure lust crashing over me with such force I almost stumble. I'm humbled, flattered, and even a little bit nervous, afraid that I won't live up to her fantasy.

Then I pause on the pool deck near our suite and simply look at her, pulling her to a stop alongside me. There's a slight wind, and the light coming from the pool is full of motion. She's drenched in it, her body glowing like some celestial creature, powerful and strong and sensual. I look down and see that I'm bathed in the same light, and in that moment, something shifts in me, and I know that whatever's between us is no longer about a teenage girl's fantasy. It's about the connection we have now. That electrical bond I've felt since the goddamn blessed day she asked me to play the part of her totally smitten fiancé.

"Gate," I say, nodding toward our garden entrance that I really can't get to fast enough. With her hand still in mine, we run like teenagers, then burst through the metal gate and let it swing closed with a clang behind us.

That's when I know I can't wait another moment. She's moved a few steps toward the French doors, but I tug her back, then press her against the ivy-covered wall. My hands slam against the stone, trapping her, and my mouth crushes hers, silencing her startled little, *oh*.

It's as if the connection lights a fuse, sending us both into a flurry of heat and desperation. Her lips part, and I explore her mouth with my tongue, tasting and biting and sucking with a wild desperation, as if I may never have the chance to do this again, and must get my fill in this moment.

She's equally desperate. Her fingers twine in my hair, keeping me pressed close, and her tongue meets mine thrust for thrust. It feels like fucking, and my cock strains against my jeans, wanting a piece of the action.

I take one hand off the wall and close it over her breast. She's wearing an off-the-shoulder blouse with no bra, and her nipple is at least as hard as my cock. I tug the elastic neck down, trapping her arms, but releasing her breasts, then shift my attention from her mouth to her tit.

"Oh, holy fuck," she whispers as I suck and bite, grazing my teeth along her nipple before sucking as much of her delicious flesh into my mouth as I can. With one hand still on the wall, I move the other to the breast I'm not currently devouring, at first just teasing her nipple, but as she responds with more and more enthusiasm, I up my game, squeezing her breast, and then pinching her nipple. Twisting it between my fingers as I lightly bite its mate.

She's trapped, nowhere to go as I undertake this sensual assault, but her body squirms and writhes, and she lifts one leg, hooking it around mine as her hips buck and she makes small whimpering sounds that to me are like gasoline on a fire, making us both burn hotter.

I lower myself, easing the blouse down to her waist as I do. "Lift your skirt," I order, and she slides her fingers out of my hair in order to comply, ruching her skirt up from the sides until it's a circle of material around her waist as well.

I pause long enough to look at her. The wall blocks the pool light and we didn't turn the porch light on, so the only illumination is from a few soft solar lights hidden among the plants. It's enough, though. Her thighs glow, and a pair of pink lacy panties cover her sex. I drop to my knees, then close my mouth over her mound, lace and all. She arches back, the movement giving me even better access to her pussy, then cries out my name.

I grin, wondering if anyone heard her and not caring if they did. She's mine, and as far as I'm concerned, everyone should know it. I slide my tongue along the edge of her panties, then use my fingers to push them aside, giving me full access to her gorgeous pussy.

"You're wet," I murmur.

"Ya think?" The words might be sarcastic, but her voice is breathy and full of desperation. "Leo, please."

"Yes, ma'am," I say, then close my mouth over her sex as I ease my fingers deep inside her. She grinds against me, moaning and begging, and though I can tell she's close, I pull back, not wanting her to go over. Not yet. Not until she's past the point of desperation.

"Leo—oh, God, Leo, *please*."

"Please, what? Touch you more? Make you come? Keep you on edge all night, until every bit of your skin tingles and the slightest whisper of wind on your pussy will send you spiraling off into the heavens."

"Yes." The word is breath. "That. All of it. Everything. But mostly, I want you. Please, Leo. I want you inside me."

Whatever plan I have to tease her mercilessly falls apart in the wake of those words and the passion in her voice. I have to have her now—have to claim her—have to bury myself deep inside her and watch her face as we both go over.

"With me," I say, drawing away as I speak and holding my hand out for her. I'd planned to take her inside, but when I see the patio chaise with the overstuffed cushions, I nod to it. "There," I say. "And I want you naked."

She practically is, what with her blouse still around her waist and her skirt half-bunched and half-falling now that she's no longer holding it up. She strips in record time, then goes to the chaise. Her eyes never leave me as she sits, not with her legs stretched out, but straddling it, her feet on the stone patio and her drenched pussy rubbing the dark green material. I wonder if she'll leave a stain. I hope she will. I want to mark this place as ours.

"Lean back," I order, easing onto the foot of the chaise. "And although I like this view, I want your legs up."

She bites her lower lip, then slips a finger down her belly. She moves her legs onto the chaise with slow, deliberate movements, all the while teasing her clit and sending me into a tailspin of desperate need.

"Careful. Keep that up and this won't last as long as you want."

"That's okay," she says, her teasing eyes on mine. "There's always round two. And three. And—"

I laugh. "I appreciate your confidence in my stamina."

"Prove me right," she demands, and that's a task I'm happy to tackle.

When she's fully on the lounger, I stand, making a show of studying every intimate inch of her. She's still playing with her clit, which is about the hottest thing ever, and I watch for a while, stroking my cock slowly until I can't stand it anymore. Then I peel off my shirt, enjoying the way her eyes roam over me as I reveal more and more skin.

"Like what you see?"

"Oh, yes."

That's about the most heartfelt compliment I've ever received, and I while I'd love to revel in her appreciation, it's her body I want more of. Her body, her touch, her desire. Hell, I want her everything, and I leave my clothes in a pile as I move to straddle the chaise so that I'm standing over her, my cock rock hard and ready.

Her lips twitch. "I like the view."

I let my eyes roam over her, taking in every exceptional inch. "So do I."

She licks her lips, and I see a tremor run through her. "Is it okay if we—" She cuts herself off with a shake of her head. "Never mind."

"What?" I try to sound casual, but I'm afraid she wants to stop or slow down, all evidence to the contrary.

"It's only that—God, Leo, I want you so much. I want to savor everything—I do. But right now, I don't want to wait anymore. Please?"

"Baby, I wouldn't dream of denying you."

I shift so that I'm no longer straddling the chaise; instead, I'm on it with her. I come closer, sliding into her welcoming arms, then case one hand down to stroke her pussy. She's so damn wet, and she moans and arches up, her whispers of "yes" and "now" going straight to my cock. And when I can't stand it anymore I gently maneuver our positions until I'm right at her core, my cock teasing her entrance while she begs me to please, please just fuck her now.

Of course, I do, filling her with one deep thrust that has her crying out even as she grabs my ass as if to push me even deeper. We move together, fast and hard, and as I get closer, I finger her clit, wanting to bring her along with me. I feel the contractions in her core as release approaches, and then she's trembling beneath me, her body breaking apart and sending me spinning off as well, following her into ecstasy until finally—finally—we make our way back from the stars and lay motionless together as the cool night air soothes our heated skin.

We stay that way for a while, then we get up and move inside, laughing softly as we wonder if anyone heard us.

"Well, we are engaged," she says, sliding naked into the bed with me.

She's on her side, and I idly trace my fingertip along the curve of her waist, not really thinking anything, just enjoying the way she looks right now.

After a moment, she meets my eyes. "Why did you?"

I shake my head, confused.

"Tonight. This." She licks her lips. "I'm not complaining, not by a long shot, and I know you're attracted to me, too. But there's the whole thing with Brody and, well, you could have said no." She glances down, her voice softer when she says, "Was it just pity after my heartfelt speech? You feeling sorry for the teenage girl trapped inside me?"

"God no," I say, wishing she could see how much I mean it.

"Then what?"

I look at her, this woman who's made it clear that this is a system cleansing. Something fleeting, but fun.

I conjure the hint of a smile. "It doesn't matter. Why analyze something that's only going to last a weekend?" I move closer so that I can slip my hand between her thighs. "Instead, let's just enjoy the time we have."

## CHAPTER ELEVEN

I STRETCH IN THE DARK, still half-asleep and not certain what sound woke me. I roll over, reaching for Sam, only to find the other side of the bed empty.

I sit up, groggy but not concerned. Last time I'd gotten bent out of shape, she'd simply been at the spa. Then I check my phone, see that it's past one in the morning, and come wide awake.

"Sam?" I keep my voice low in case she's asleep in the other room. Maybe she got up last night after we made love, then went in there to read and fell asleep. But as soon as I go into the sitting area, I see that's not the case.

I also see that the drapes are moving, caught in a breeze that isn't coming from the AC vent. I pull the curtain aside and find the door cracked open. Since that probably means that Sam is out in the garden, I step outside as well. But she's not here either, and when I go to the gate, I see that it's firmly closed.

Frowning, I unlatch the gate, then step into the poolside common area. A single light is on, and waves of watery light ripple over the area, providing just enough illumination to make out the other suites.

I turn slowly, taking in the area, but see no one. Maybe she's with Cherry? That's what women do before a wedding, right? And the ceremony is tomorrow, after all.

I'm surprised she didn't tell me she'd be leaving, but maybe it was a last minute thing. Feeling somewhat better, I head back into the garden, intending to give up and go back inside, when I see a flicker of movement on the far side of the pool. I look again, trying to make it out, then realize it's a figure moving in the shadows near the entrance to Reg's suite.

*Surely that's not...*

But it is. I recognize her as soon as a glimmer of pool light hits her. Her eyes wide and her face flushed.

I wait inside the gate, and as soon as she steps through, I take her arm and pull her toward me, clapping my other hand over her mouth to quiet her bloodcurdling scream.

"What the hell?" Her whisper is low and angry when I finally release her.

"I think that's a question for me," I retort as soon as

I've tugged her inside the suite and shut the door. "What the hell were you doing sneaking out of Reg's suite?"

Her eyes go wide. "You cannot possibly think that I went over there for a quickie. Oh my God, Leo. Ewww."

I release her arm. "God no," I say, because if she's still interested in Reg, then I need to forget about doing investigative work, because I saw not one iota of evidence. "I think you're stealing corporate secrets."

She'd been in a defensive posture, ready to challenge whatever came out of my mouth. But now she cringes back, as if I'd struck a hard blow across her cheek.

A cold steel band tightens around my heart. "Fuck." My word is soft, but the emotion is severe. I leave her standing there as I pace the sitting area, frustrated because the furniture is too damn prissy to punch or kick without breaking something. "*Fuck.*"

This time, it's a yell, and I see her jump. I don't care. I really don't. "You used me," I say, crossing back to her. "All weekend, Reg has chattered about his industry and corporate spies. The same goddamn industry you're freelancing in. Does stealing secrets pay better than contract labor?"

I expect her to yell right back at me. To get completely defensive. I even expect there'll be tears.

What I don't expect is the hard, fiery slap she lands on my left cheek.

"You raging bastard," she says, the words low and measured. "Do you really think I'd do that?"

"No." The word is automatic, said without thinking. But it's true, and I can tell that she knows it, too, because I see the relief in her eyes. "No, I don't. But what were you doing in there? And dammit, why didn't you tell me?"

My words melt the last bit of steel inside her, and she sinks down onto a mauve ottoman. "I didn't know if you'd help me."

"Baby, where have you been?" I kneel in front of her, my hands on her knees. "I will always help you."

"Easy to say without knowing the story."

"Always," I repeat firmly. "But tell me, anyway."

She draws in a breath, then nods. "Okay," she says, but before she can start, I hush her with a finger over her lip. "Does this change any of what you said before?"

"About you?" The corner of her mouth curves up in what I think is relief. "Not a single word."

"Good. Go on."

"We did work together at MT," she begins. "But it didn't end quite the way I said. There was a gap when neither of us worked for another company. That's when we started dating and when we started our own company. Unfortunately, we did the work before we drew up the papers, so the whole thing was kind of a mess."

She continues, telling me how she worked for months refining a next-level operating system geared toward gaming. "I'd been brainstorming it for years but never had enough time to dig deep. So while I did that, Reg started making contacts. Putting the pieces in place for our big jump into the market."

"Let me guess. That's when he met Lisa."

She nods, then tells me about how he cheated on her with Lisa, specifically not breaking up until after the system was essentially complete. "But we had a partnership, even if the paperwork was dicey. And we both had access to the server that held all our system files."

I clench my fists, pretty sure I see where this is going.

"He offered to buy me out." She tells me the number, and I whistle. "I know. It's a lot. But not even close to what it was worth then or what he'll get selling it to Sunspot. But the truth is that I was tired of him. Tired of the whole thing, really. So I agreed, and he paid me half. I used part of it to buy the Crestview house."

"But somewhere we make a left turn."

She nods. "Around the time of the sale, he hacked

my computer. Came over for coffee one day supposedly to go over details of the sale of the business and sign the contract, since if nothing else he'd need that in writing if he wanted to license it up the chain. Later, when I was out of the room, he logged onto my laptop and locked me out of everything."

"He knew your password."

"He knew everything. Either because he had legitimate access through the business or because he'd paid attention while we were sleeping together. I don't tell anyone my passwords. Ever. But he has a photographic memory. If I was nearby when I logged in..."

"Yeah," I say. "I get it. But what does this have to do with tonight?"

"His big presentation on Monday—the one he's been bragging about that's supposed to nail him a promotion—is for our system."

I frown, processing all of that. "So the corporate spies he's worried about—that's you?" She already told me she wasn't spying tonight, but maybe Reg thought she would?

"Hell no. Why would I need to spy? It's already in my head and notes. If I had to, I could rebuild it."

"Then I'm not following."

"He paid me half. *Half*. He's arranged a life-changing, career making meeting for himself on a system that he got through larceny. As far as I'm concerned, he's climbing the ladder on my goodwill. And I don't have a lot of goodwill to spare for that prick."

"You want more money?"

She shakes her head. "I want what he agreed to. And I want it before he sells what doesn't really belong to him."

"But the meeting's tomorrow," I point out, because it's technically Sunday now.

"I know. That's why I was in his suite. I was trying to hack into the system and install a paywall."

"A—wait. You were going to set it up so that he's stuck until he pays?"

"Yup. I have everything all set up. He just has to log in and authorize the transfer. The money will hit my account immediately, and within minutes, he'll have access to the system again."

"So where was Reg tonight?"

She lifts a shoulder, unconcerned. "Asleep. He takes meds. Once he's out, it's forever."

"Dammit, Sam. What if he skipped his meds tonight?" My voice is probably harsher than it should be, but I've seen a lot of shit in my time, and the knowledge of what might have happened to her makes my blood run cold.

She reaches over and takes my hand. "I'm sorry I didn't tell you the truth from the very beginning."

"And I'm sorry I jumped to conclusions."

We share a smile. "So that's the story of how I got screwed by my ex."

"Screwed," I repeat, then focus on a detail from earlier. "You said you *tried* to install the paywall. What happened?"

"He'd changed things up enough that I couldn't get through."

"Then? Or ever?"

"What does it matter? Tomorrow's the wedding, and he's not even staying the night. He'll be off to Austin after the ceremony. I could go back in tonight, but I don't think I could pull everything I need together by morning." She shakes her head in disgust.

"Maybe it's for the best. He'd be one hell of an enemy if you humiliate him in a board meeting. He might even sue you, and even if he doesn't win, it would be a pain in the ass."

"No, no. He deserves it, but I wasn't intending anyone at Sunspot to know about this. He always double and triple checks things. He'll probably do a test run after the wedding before he drives back and another one in his office before the big meeting. I figured my bank account would be full before you even dropped me back at my house."

I stand up, then extend my hand. She takes it, and I pull her into a hug. "Then let's make that happen."

"What?" She pushes back, studying my face. "How?"

"I don't know yet, but this is the kind of thing that I do. Congratulations, baby. You're our newest client."

# CHAPTER TWELVE

"SOUNDS like the best time to get in is during the wedding," Cayden says.

We're in The Oak Room on Main Street, this time sitting in a corner around a cocktail table made from a wine barrel. Cayden and I are sipping bourbon and Sam is toying with her red wine, having barely touched it.

"And you're sure you can do this?" I don't need to hear the nerves in her voice to know how on edge she is about this plan. This is, after all, the fifth time she's asked that question since we met Cayden two hours ago.

I'd called him this morning to explain the situation. Since Pierce is still out of town and Connor and Kerrie are using weekends for their own wedding planning, Cayden was the natural choice.

"Have I gotten anything wrong so far?"

She shakes her head. They'd been using her laptop to run a simulation she created overnight, and so far he's aced it, using the tricks and tools she described to him.

"It's just different when you're in that room alone," she says.

"I promise you I can handle it." With the patch, Cayden can come off scary if he wants to. Right now, he's nothing but gentle reassurance. "I've got mad tech skills. More than that, I have step by step instructions from you and a genius in my back pocket."

"Huh?"

"The firm partners with a tech genius at the Austin office of Stark Applied Technology," I tell her. "It's how we get our best gadgets."

Cayden pulls his phone from his back pocket. "Got him on speed dial. Seriously, do you think this clown would put you in my hands if he didn't think I could do it?"

Sam's eyes go to mine, and for a moment it's just the two of us. "No," she whispers. "He wouldn't."

"All right, then," Cayden says, flashing a winning smile. "Let's start digging down. Wedding's at sunset. I want you to quiz me on the hack at least a dozen times before that, with every worst case scenario you can think of."

She nods. "I have the bridal tea in a few, but when I get back, we'll jump into that. In the meantime, memorize the notes I gave you."

Cayden nods. "You got it, boss."

"How did you get into his room?" I ask, realizing we'd left out that little detail.

"I just waited until no one was at reception and stole the extra key."

Cayden laughs. "Yeah, you'll do," he says, and I actually swell with pride.

"You brought coms?" I ask him.

"Not my first rodeo, remember? Of course I did."

"Good. If you need any specific help, Sam can fake a stomach bug and head to the ladies room."

"Are you just going to wander into the resort?" Sam asks him. "Won't people wonder?"

"I've got a gardener's uniform in my truck. And I don't wander. In and out. Won't be a problem."

"Okay then." She sucks in air, then lets it out again. "I guess—well, I guess I'll let you guys go over stuff on your own and I'll be back after the bridal tea so we can work through it some more."

She stands, as do Cayden and I. She gives me an awkward hug that I translate as *I have no idea if I can kiss you in front of this guy*, then accepts Cayden's bear hug.

With one last look at me, she heads out the door,

and not for the first time, I hope this last minute, pulled-out-of-our-asses mission will go through. Because I can't stand the thought of failing and disappointing her.

"All right," Cayden says once she's out of sight. "I want the blow by blow."

A few days ago, I might have told him to fuck off. Today, I tell him the entire story, glossing over nothing except the most intimate of details.

"So there you go," I say, not sure if I actually want advice or just needed to unburden. "And if you breathe a word of this to Brody, you're a dead man."

"My lips are sealed, except to offer you advice."

"I'm listening."

"Go out, find a woman, and fuck her until you get your mind off that one."

"What the hell?"

Cayden leans back, then takes a sip of whiskey before answering. "That's your MO, right? And you like this girl. So stop while you're ahead. Don't risk breaking her heart because you're only interested in fucking around."

He's partly right, of course. That used to be the way I operated. But now? Now I hardly recognize that man.

I sip my own drink, then trace a pattern in the condensation on the tabletop. "I look at you and

Gracie, and Connor and Kerrie, and Pierce and Jez, and I wonder what the fuck I was doing playing hopscotch over women, landing on one just long enough to launch myself to the next."

"That presents a terrible mental picture. You know that right?"

I ignore him.

"Do you know why before last weekend I hadn't slept with a woman in over two months?"

"Because you'd already run through the entire single population of Austin?"

"Funny. No, it's because I hadn't met one that I *didn't* want to fuck. And I don't mean that in the *I wouldn't want her in my bed* kind of way. I mean that I hadn't met a woman special enough to make me want more than just entertainment between the sheets."

I pause, swirling my glass so the single ice cube clinks against the sides. "I hadn't met a single woman I'd like to take to dinner and simply talk with. Then take her home and kiss her good night, and go home happy because it was a good date, and I wanted another one, and another one after that, and then a few more besides, all paving the path to the bedroom, sure. But when we got there it would mean something."

"Are you saying that's Sam?"

"I don't—" I frown. "Yeah, I think I am."

"Think? Sure sounds definite to me."

"Then I really am fucked—and not in a good way. Because she only wants me for the fantasy potential."

"You sure about that? Not the vibe I was getting just now."

"She's very clear. Her life is in Seattle, and I'm the childhood fantasy she wants to spend the weekend fucking out of her system."

He makes a grunting sound.

"What?"

"Just that in my experience women don't always say what they want. Neither do men, to be fair." He taps a coaster on the table. "Actually, okay, the truth is, in my experience nobody ever says what they want."

"Do you have a point?"

"A point? Yes, my friend, I do. Pull that particular stick out of your ass, and who knows what you'll end up with? Don't, and you've got no one to blame but yourself."

## CHAPTER THIRTEEN

THE WEDDING IS BEAUTIFUL, but I don't think either Sam or I really notice. We're too lost in our own thoughts and fears. I know I am, anyway. Thoughts about Sam. Fear that Cayden will get caught.

Fear that I'll never see her again.

As for Sam, I don't know what she's thinking, but I do see her frequently brush her hair back behind the ear with the com link in it. And I see the way her brows furrow, as if she's worried that Cayden isn't really sailing along in blissful radio silence, but is shouting for help that she's not hearing.

I reach over and take her hand, gratified when she shoots me a quick, nervous smile.

She keeps her fingers twined with mine for the rest of the ceremony, only releasing me after the newly pronounced Mr. and Mrs. Tarrant walk back down the aisle together, this time accepting hugs and handshakes and congratulations.

"You looked beautiful," Sam tells Cherry, wrapping her friend in a hug.

"You'll be next," Cherry says, glancing at me with a grin, and I notice that although Sam blushes, she doesn't meet my eye.

I have absolutely no clue how to interpret that.

And I can't even ask Cayden, who's just texted me the all clear. As per the plan, that means he's heading back to Austin, and Sam and I are left to wait and see if our cobbled-together plan really worked.

A huge white tent has been erected on the property, complete with a polished wooden floor, a partitioned-off dance area, over a dozen small tables for eating and conversation, the gift and appetizer table, a bandstand, and, of course, a bar.

We've just been through the bar line and as soon as we grab one of the tables, Sam turns to me. "He said it went well?"

"All done, all good, and he's on his way home."

"Right. Okay." She fans herself with the souvenir program that's at each place setting. "I wasn't nervous before but now I'm a wreck."

I take her hand again, then kiss her wrist. "It'll work. And we'll know soon. Tonight, right?"

She nods, then shakes her head. "Probably. I don't

know. Whenever he decides to test it." She runs her fingers through her hair, the movement making the subtle red highlights shine in the soft tent lighting. "Reg is standing right over there. What if he stays here to the bitter end? He'll probably just wait and test tomorrow at the office."

"Then we'll know tomorrow," I say.

"Right. I know. Sorry. I don't mean to spazz out."

"Spazz all you want. I'll be right here to hold your hand."

She tilts her head as if studying me, her brow furrowing. "Will you?"

My heart hitches, and the word is out before I can think about it. "Always," I say. More than that, I mean it.

"I guess so. That's what you and Brody promised, right? That one or the other of you would always be there for me."

I frown, something in her tone giving me pause. "Well, yes, but—"

"We don't have to stop." She blurts the words out with such force I'm surprised the couple at the table nearest us doesn't ask what we're talking about. "Sorry," she whispers. "I just—I've been trying to figure out how to say this. And, well, I'm going to dive in and start talking."

I nod, but say nothing, afraid I'll get her off track.

"I know we go back to reality tomorrow, and, well, first I want to say thank you. For making my fantasy come true."

"Sure," I say, but I have to force the word out past the giant lump that's suddenly lodged in my gut. A hard mass of regret and recrimination, and even loss. Because, dammit, I'm already ten steps down this road, and the destination isn't where I'd hoped to end up.

"I guess what I want to say is that we don't have to stop."

I wait a beat, then say slowly, "What do you mean?"

"My project got cancelled. The freelance gig here. So I'm going home. Back to Seattle."

*Home? Seattle is not Sam's home.*

I don't say that, though. Instead, I ask, "When?"

"Five days."

"Five days?" This really isn't computing. "What about your flip?"

"Brody's going to come down and help me finish off what I already started. Then he said he'd manage it if I want to turn it into a rental. I figure that's a solid plan for the time being, and it's good for him, too. He's taking a leave of absence from the company, and I have a feeling his CEO days are numbered."

That's about the only good news I've heard so far. "What do you think he'll do?"

"No idea. Maybe go back to being a cop? Anyway, the point is that this—" She gestures to the resort. "All of this was a box. Our time here—the things we've done —they've been in the Fredericksburg box. Limited, I mean. And now ... well we can keep on. If you want to. Because it would still be limited. Five more days, just a different location. It would still have to be a secret, but that can be fun, too, right?"

She bites her lower lip, her pupils moving as she studies me, obviously trying to read my face.

But I can keep my emotions in check when I want to, and right now, I don't want to reveal a single, goddamn thing.

"I mean, if you want to," she adds lamely. "It's only —well, you know I've fantasized about you forever. And I've had a really good time during our pretend engagement."

"So have I," I say sincerely, even as that rock weighs down my gut. "And I'm thrilled I lived up to your expectations." I pause, not quite believing I'm really going to say it. "But no."

"No?"

"I'm sorry. I just—no."

Her mouth forms an O, but she says nothing. Then her lips tighten into something like a smile. "Right. Of course. It's silly. We had fun. Why risk ruining those memories?"

I haven't got a clue what to say. That I want her to stay? That I want to be more than a lingering teenage fantasy? That I want to be the man she wants and not the memory she covets?

But she's going home, and I'm tired of spinning my wheels.

And I don't know how to say any of that. So I bend over to kiss her forehead, then stand up. "I'm going to take a walk. Text me when he leaves?"

"Oh." She takes a deep breath, then nods. "Yeah. Sure. Of course, I will."

## CHAPTER FOURTEEN

I WALK with no plan other than trying to wrap my head around the fact that this is the end. But it's not working. Sam's gotten under my skin in a way no other woman ever has. It's only been days, but I can't imagine her not being in my life. Or in my bed.

Did she truly only want me for the fantasy? A mental cleansing before she goes back to her life?

I don't think so. Everything in her voice—in her touch—suggests something more. Something deeper.

But I don't know the truth, and she's leaving.

Which means that unless I get my shit together and find out one way or another, I might end up losing the best thing that ever happened to me.

And since I'm not prepared to let that happen, it's time to take the leap.

With a silent prayer, I pull out my phone, then dial Brody's number.

He answers on the first ring. "Hey, man, I was just thinking of you. How's it going?"

"Actually, I'm in love with your sister." Nothing like getting straight to the point.

"Are you?" The boisterous tone is replaced with the even, steady voice of an investigating officer. "And her? Is she in love with you?"

"That's what I need to find out. I'm about to throw myself out there to the wolves, and figured I'd start with you." I clear my throat. "She didn't say anything about me when you guys last talked, did she?"

"Not a word. We only talked about the house. You heard about the move?"

"Yup."

"And that prompted this call?"

"I don't want to lose her. Not if there's a chance. But, dammit, I don't know if she just wanted a fling with her high school crush or if there's something more underneath."

"Wanted," he repeats. "That would be past tense."

"Are you sure? I seem to recall you getting a D in freshman English."

"Ah, hell." I can practically hear him rubbing the back of his neck. Then I hear him suck in a breath. "Well, I always suspected she had a crush. But Sam holds things close to the vest. If she's saying she only wanted a fling, maybe she did. But what the hell do I know? You have literally just dumped on me more information about my sister's sex life than I ever knew or wanted to know."

"All I said was that she wanted a fling and that I've fallen in love."

"Like I said, that first part is more than I need to know. The second part ... well, if you're sure, then I'm happy for you. I've only been in love once, and although I'd probably hurt a lot less now if I never had been, I wouldn't change it for the world."

"I know. I get it." I exhale. "So I'm forgiven?"

"What, for breaking your promise? Hell no. That's solid currency for decades between us. But you have my blessing to talk to her. And more than that, I'm rooting for you. When are you going to tell her?"

"Actually, I was thinking right now."

———

I burst into the suite ready to tell her everything, but before I get a word out, she looks up from where she's sitting at the small table, her computer open in front of her.

"We're on," she says, her eyes wide with excitement.

"He's running the test?" I hurry to her, then pull up a chair so that I can see the screen as well. The code that she gave Cayden hijacks the computer's camera, turning it on without the indicator light going live. Which means that we're looking at a split screen. On one side, the main system page that he's just logged into. On the other, his face—flush with concentration—as he navigates through the demo of the operating system that he'll be showing his boss tomorrow.

"Two more screens to go," Sam whispers, reaching out to grab my hand.

He clicks to the next screen, and I watch his eyes skim over the display. Another click, and the same quick skim.

He clicks again, and because I know it's coming, I'm looking right at Reg's face when his eyes go wide and his mouth drops open. There's no sound, but I can practically hear his, "Oh, no. Oh, fuck no," from across the pool.

"What if he comes over?" There's fear in her voice. "He knows it's me."

"Then I'll handle him. But he won't. He knows the situation as well as you do. Better. And right now, he's the only one with anything at stake."

I see him mouth, "Bitch," and for a moment consider going over there and punching the guy. I say nothing, but my thoughts must show on my face, because she pats my hand and says simply, "Down, boy."

At that moment, Sam's phone chirps and a text message flashes simultaneously on her computer.

*Reg: You didn't have to go to extremes.*

She types back:

*Sam: Yeah. I did.*

*Reg: I'm the wrong person for you to cross in this industry. I have a lot of power at Sunspot.*

*Sam: Maybe I don't care about being in this industry.*

There's no reply, but Reg is hunched over the computer.

"Is he trying to hack past the wall?"

Her shoulders rise and fall. "Probably."

The phone dings again, and I scan the computer screen, looking for the corresponding text. But there's nothing there.

Sam's smile, however, is wider than I've ever seen it.

"Was that—?"

"Payment notification," she says, then grabs up her phone, flips through screens, pauses, then does a fist pump. "Yes!"

She tosses the phone onto the table, shoves back her chair, and it's only when she leaps into my arms that I realize I'm already standing.

Her mouth closes over mine, and I revel in the fast, hard kiss. At least until she gasps, then starts to push back with, "Sorry. I shouldn't have—"

"Wait." I hold her tight, not letting her leave the circle of my arms. "Just hold up a second. I need to say something. The truth is that I don't want to do some pretend hidden relationship with you. But it's not because I don't want you. It's because I *do*. I want reality, not pretend. Because, here's the thing, Sam. I've fallen in love with you."

She stares at me. One beat, then another in total, ominous silence.

And then she bursts into tears.

*Shit.*

"It's okay," I hurry to say. "It's okay if you don't feel the same way. No pressure, but I had to tell you, because—"

She cuts me off with a shove and a laugh. "No, you freak. These are happy tears." She flings her arms around me. "Thank you. Thank you for being braver then me. I couldn't — I thought you didn't want anything more. When you turned me down at the reception, I thought that was it. You were done. That I was just a favor to Brody topped off with a gift of wish fulfillment for me and a nice little hook-up for you. And I told myself that everything I felt between us was wishful thinking on my part."

"It was real," I say. "It *is* real. I've never felt—oh, fuck it. I don't want you to go to Seattle, okay? I want to let what's between us grow, because I think there's something special here, and I want you to stay here where my friends are and where your brother is. And maybe we can even make that crazy house you're flipping into something special together."

She starts to speak, but my words are still bubbling out.

"But if your work is back there, then go. Just know that I'm going to follow you."

"No—"

"Yes. I will."

She laughs. "I mean, no. I don't want to go back. I did, but that was before."

"Before what?"

"Before I realized that I'm tired of that industry. Before I figured out what I want."

"What's that?"

"You," she said, melting my heart.

"You mean us."

She nods, her eyes sparkling with tears. "I love you, too," she whispers, "I think I always have."

Then she rises on her toes as she hooks her arms around my neck. Our lips meet, and I lose myself in a long, slow kiss that tastes a little bit like strawberries, and a lot like the future.

# EPILOGUE

*Five months later*

"YOU'RE TEMPTING ME," I tell the perfect, naked woman standing in her bedroom—*our* bedroom as of last Friday.

Sam turns from her dressing table, holding a pair of lacy pink panties. She's not wearing a bra, and she crosses her arms over her chest, as if hiding the sight of those perfect tits will put me off at all.

I stalk toward her, and she laughs as she backs away, but with the table a few inches behind her, there's really nowhere to go. "Don't you dare. I just did my make-up, and Brody'll be here in fifteen minutes."

"Plenty of time," I say, pulling her hands away and replacing them with my own.

Her lips part, and I don't wait to find out if she's

going to cry out with pleasure or order me to stop so she can finish getting dressed. I close my mouth over hers, twisting her nipples so that she moans against my mouth before gently pulling away.

"Leo..."

"Plenty of time," I repeat as I take her by the waist and lift her up onto the desk-style table, right in front of the padded stool where her bare ass has perched so many times.

"We can't," she says, but she's leaning back, her arms behind her for balance as she spreads her legs for me, revealing her sweet, bare pussy.

"That's right," I say, as I settle onto the stool, then lazily trail my index finger up the soft skin inside her thigh.

"Oh..."

The word, so soft with pleasure, shoots through me. I want to draw this out. To push her to the edge, then throw her on the bed and bury myself inside her.

But that will have to wait. She's right—company soon. And right now, all I want to do is make the woman I love shatter.

With deliberate slowness, I let my mouth follow my finger's path, using the tip of my tongue to lightly tease until she's squirming with pleasure and begging me to touch her.

If we had more time, I'd take all afternoon. As it is,

I only have minutes. She's already wet, and I tease her folds, dipping my finger in and out as I kiss my way to her clit, then suck on that sweet nub as she goes wild, her hips shifting with the rhythm of my thrusts.

She tastes like heaven and her soft moans are definitely making me even harder. I know she's close—I can feel the muscles of her core tightening around the fingers that are teasing her so intimately. I slide in deeper, sucking harder, using my tongue to tease her just so as she squirms and gasps and—

"That's it, baby. Come for me, Samantha."

As if on command, she shatters around me, her cry rivaling the sharp chime of the doorbell.

"Shit," she says, her body still convulsing. "That was incredible, but shit, fuck, shit."

I laugh, my finger still inside her, teasing the last tremor out of her.

"Stop. Oh my god, Brody has a key. Leo, stop."

I do, and she sighs, then pulls me up to kiss her. "I lied," she says, closing her knees to trap me between her legs. "Never stop."

"Never," I promise.

"You're mine, mister. Forever."

"'Til death do us part," I say. "After all, isn't Brody taking us out to celebrate our engagement?"

"Yes," she says. "And that means you need to go let him in while I get dressed."

"I'm a little rumpled," I say, glancing at my shirt.

"Your own fault. Go."

I take one lingering look at my beautiful, naked fiancée—real, this time—then head through the house toward the door. It's the Crestview house, now almost completely renovated. We're keeping it for now. Although someday I hope we'll have one or two reasons to upsize.

I cross the living area, then pull open the new wood and glass door to let in Brody.

"I can't believe my best friend's marrying my sister. Now you're probably going to go and have kids."

"It's a crazy ass world," I say. "But yeah, that's on the agenda."

"Good. Get on that. I'll make a stellar uncle."

"Give us a few more years," Sam says, crossing the room to give her brother a hug. "I want time to enjoy having wild sex in the living room without the pitter patter of little feet."

"I cannot begin to tell you how much I did not need to hear that."

"Don't worry, big brother. You'll be an uncle someday." She takes his hand. "And at least we're not separated by half the country anymore. Just a couple hundred miles."

Brody is still officially on leave, but since Sam

didn't need him to help with the house, he stayed in Dallas.

"That's not nearly close enough. How will I pop in to bother you two at the most inconvenient times? Or when you do have kids, how can I properly spoil them rotten all the way from North Texas? For that matter," he adds, hooking his thumb toward me, "how can I keep an eye on this one to make sure he's treating you right?"

I shake my head, amused.

"I'm sure you'll figure out a way," she teases. "You're very resourceful."

"I am," he says, the corners of his eyes crinkling the way they always do when he's telling a joke but hasn't yet come to the punch line. "That's why I put in an offer on a house four blocks over."

"No shit?"

"That's fabulous!" Sam squeals, then hugs him again. "When did you decide to move down here?"

"About the time I accepted a job."

"Congratulations," I say. "Where are you landing?"

"Your neck of the woods, actually. I just signed on at Blackwell-Lyon."

The End

Thanks so much for reading *Tempting Little Tease*. Be sure to keep an eye out for Brody's book, *Dirty Little Devil*, coming soon! (Hint: visit my website to sign up for my newsletter — www.jkenner.com—or text **JKenner** to **21000** to be notified of all new releases!

And now, something special for you! This Bonus Content is the deleted first chapter from my original draft. Enjoy!

———

"Leo, you copy? Are you in place?" Pierce's low voice whispers from my earpiece, and I click the mic twice to acknowledge my position.

"Cayden?"

"Roger, that. I'm in position and ready to follow if the bastard makes it past Palermo."

That's me, Leonardo Vincent Palermo, and I click the mic once in protest against the idea that there is any chance in hell that Rufus Dorne will get his thieving, sniveling carcass past me.

On the line, I hear a chuckle and assume it's Cayden, who knows damn well I want to call him out, but that I have to stay silent as I'm currently tucked inside the coat closet in the office of our client, waiting for our suspect to make an appearance.

I've been working this case for the last two months of my four month tenure at Blackwell-Lyon Security, ever since my best friend, Brody Carrington, recommended our services to his friend Gary Crane, the right hand of one of the United States' senators from Texas. The Senator's ramping up for re-election. And Gary suspects there's someone on staff selling his secrets and strategies.

It only took a few weeks on the case to confirm the breach, and soon after that we had our eye on three potential suspects, with the good money on Dorne.

Today's all about the cat catching that particular mouse.

The closet is stuffy and smells of sweat and peppermint, presumably from Gary's habit of constantly popping breath mints. I've been in here for almost an hour and am tempted to crack the door to let in some breathable air.

I hold back, though, and am immediately relieved that I did when I hear the sharp *click* of a key turning in Gary's office door.

I smile and think, *Meow*.

"The mouse is in the house." This time the voice belongs to Connor, Cayden's twin, who is operating the zoom and pan features of the video equipment we installed to survey the interior of this room and the hall outside. "Let's see if he goes for the cheese."

With Connor at the controls, Cayden watching Dorne's car, and Pierce overseeing the operation as a whole, it falls on me to actually take the bastard down. Now, I use my phone to log into the room's video feed, giving me the perspective of looking over Dorne's shoulder.

"Fucker," Connor says as he tightens focus on the camera aimed at the desk. "And ballsy, too. He just used his own thumbprint to log onto Gary's laptop. You can bet that wasn't authorized."

"He's tightening his own noose," Cayden says, voicing my thoughts. Gary has a program installed on his computer that tracks log-ins. With an alphanumeric passcode, there's no way to know who, only when. But with biometrics...

"True," Pierce says. "And oh—*fuck*."

I tense as image after image pops onto Gary's monitor, clearly being copied off the flashdrive that Dorne has connected to the machine. Porn, and despite the speed with which the images zip by, it's easy to tell that most of the girls are very, very underage.

"He's setting Gary up," Cayden says. "The discovery of those files on his computer will completely overshadow the allegations of theft."

I couldn't agree more, and I'm itching to burst from my post. But this is Pierce's mission, and so I wait, my phone back in my pocket, my hand on my weapon, until—

"We're clear," Connor says. "We've got everything locked in on vid including a shot of his face. He's not worming his way out of this."

"Leo, go," Pierce orders, and the words aren't even out of his mouth before I've burst into the open, my weapon aimed at Dorne, and my cry of *"Freeze,"* echoing in the dimly lit room.

He looks up, his bushy brows rising to reveal eyes filled with shock—but not fear.

"Don't shoot, man," he says.

"Hands up. We need to have a little chat."

He nods, moving slowly as he starts to comply. Then he puts on a burst of speed, grabs Gary's metal desk chair, and starts to spin toward the window behind the desk.

"*Shit.*" The curse flies from my lips even as I fire a warning shot. It bursts through the window at the same time as the desk chair shatters the glass, and Dorne leaps through a second later, dropping out of sight.

My weapon is holstered, and I'm across the room before I even have time to utter another curse.

"Balcony," Connor says. "One level below. Glad I mounted cameras on the roof."

I look down, but see only darkness.

"Is there a way off or will he double back inside?" The cameras are infrared, which is good since I can't see a thing through the thick darkness of the night.

"Fire escape," Connor says. "Ladder mounted to the brick off to the south side. He's already hoisting tail over the rail. If you double back through the inside, you'll miss him."

And so I jump—hoping to hell that Connor is right. That there is a balcony, and that it really is only one story below us.

I get my answer when I land almost immediately with a thud on the polished concrete of this fifth floor balcony.

A tiny light is embedded in the bricks just over the balcony rail, and as my eyes adjust, I realize that it exists to mark the location of the fire escape. I go to that side, hold onto the concrete rail, and peer over.

I can't make out any features, but there is definitely

a figure scurrying down the ladder—and he's got a significant head start.

With Pierce and Cayden and Connor urging me on, I climb over rail, then reach for the closest vertical post. As soon as I have a grip, I hoist myself up onto the rail, swing my feet over, then carefully maneuver one foot onto the perpendicular rung. Another second, and both feet are on the ladder and both hands are clutching the vertical supports. One more breath, and I'm climbing down.

"This guy's a monkey," Pierce says. "He's almost to the ground. Cayden, be ready to tail him. He's going to jump in about five feet, hit the ground, then bolt, and—"

"The hell he is," I say, kicking off my shoes so I'm only in my socks. I loosen my grip with my hands, move my feet to the outside of the vertical posts, and let myself slide down the ladder, just like I used to do on the playground as a kid.

*Thwaaaap!*

I land on the guy with all the force of my downward acceleration. He makes a yelping noise, falls the final few feet, then hits the ground with a thud.

I hang onto the ladder with my left hand, and use my right to pull my Glock free of my shoulder holster. I descend the rest of the way, keeping a tight aim on

Rufas Dorne's chest as I hit the ground. I move to stand beside him, meeting his angry eyes.

"And that, gentlemen," I say into the mic, "wraps up a job well done."

## MEET PIERCE IN LOVELY LITTLE LIAR

**_She's not the woman I thought ... but dammit, she's the woman I want._**

I never thought of myself as cynical, but getting dumped at the altar changes a man.

Now, I'm all about my job. About building my business and getting on with my life. Don't get me wrong; I still love women. I love the way they look. The way they smell. The way they feel. Especially the way they feel. And I've pretty much made it my mission to give each and every woman who shares my bed the ride of her life.

But getting close? Getting serious? Giving a woman my trust again? Yeah, that's not going to happen.

Or so I thought.

Then I met her. It's funny how things can change in a heartbeat. How one case of mistaken identity can change everything. But there she was, all business and completely uninterested in me. And damned if I didn't want her. Crave her.

Most of all, I wanted to help her. To keep her and her sister safe. But the more I get to know her, the more I want her. The whole package. The complete woman.

And the miracle is that she wants me, too.

Trouble is, we've both been burned before. Now, I know one thing for certain—the only way that we'll survive the heat that crackles between us is if we both find the courage to leap into the fire together.

*Lovely Little Liar is a novella originally published as Bitch Slap. Minor edits, such as expanded scenes, have been made to this book.*

## Meet Cayden in Pretty Little Player

*Bedroom games are fine ... but I need a woman who won't play with my heart.*

After years in the military, I've faced down a lot of things, and there's not much I shy away from. Except relationships. Because when you catch your wife in bed with another man, that tends to sour even the most hardened man against women.

When I was hired to keep surveillance on a woman with a checkered past, I went into the job anticipating the worst. But what I found was a woman who turned my head. Who made my blood heat and my body burn. A woman who made me feel alive again.

A woman who was nothing like what I expected, but everything I wanted. A woman who, it turned out, needed my protection. And wanted my touch.

And as the world fell out from under us, and everything I thought I knew shifted, there was only one reality I could hold onto—that the more I got to know her, the more I wanted her.

But if I'm going to make her mine, I'll have to not only keep her safe, I'll have to prove to her that I've conquered my own fears and doubts. That I'm done looking into the past, and that all I want is a future —with her.

## Meet Connor in Sexy Little Sinner

***It was wrong to stay together ... but we couldn't stay apart.***

I've been with my share of women, but none touched my heart and fired my senses the way she did. Her smile enticed me. Her caresses teased me. Her body aroused me.

And yet, it couldn't last. There were too many years between us. A gap we couldn't breach, and we broke it off. No. *I* broke it off. And I've regretted that decision ever since.

Now she's in danger, and there's no one else I trust to protect her. But the more time we spend together, the more I want her back. And all I know now is I have to keep her safe—and despite both of us knowing better, somehow, someway, she will be mine again.

## Who's Your Man of the Month?

When a group of fiercely determined friends realize their beloved hang-out is in danger of closing, they take matters into their own hands to bring back customers lost to a competing bar. Fighting fire with a heat of their own, they double down with the broad shoulders, six-pack abs, and bare chests of dozens of hot, local guys who they cajole, prod, and coerce into auditioning for a Man of the Month calendar.

But it's not just the fate of the bar that's at stake. Because as things heat up, each of the men meets his match in this sexy, flirty, and compelling binge-read romance series of twelve novels releasing every other week from *New York Times* bestselling author J. Kenner.

"With each novel featuring a favorite romance trope— beauty and the beast, billionaire bad boys, friends to lovers, second chance romance, secret baby, and more —[the Man of the Month] series hits the heart and soul of romance." *New York Times* bestselling author Carly Phillips

**Down On Me - Hold On Tight - Need
You Now**
**Start Me Up - Get It On - In Your Eyes**
**Turn Me On - Shake It Up - All Night Long**
**In Too Deep - Light My Fire - Walk The Line**

**Bar Bites: A Man of the Month Cookbook**

# ABOUT THE AUTHOR

J. Kenner (aka Julie Kenner) is the *New York Times*, *USA Today*, *Publishers Weekly*, *Wall Street Journal* and #1 International bestselling author of over one hundred novels, novellas and short stories in a variety of genres.

JK has been praised by *Publishers Weekly* as an author with a "flair for dialogue and eccentric characterizations" and by *RT Bookclub* for having "cornered the market on sinfully attractive, dominant antiheroes and the women who swoon for them." A six-time finalist for Romance Writers of America's prestigious RITA award, JK took home the first RITA trophy awarded in the category of erotic romance in 2014 for her novel, *Claim Me* (book 2 of her Stark Saga) and the RITA trophy for *Wicked Dirty* in the same category in 2017.

In her previous career as an attorney, JK worked as a lawyer in Southern California and Texas. She currently lives in Central Texas, with her husband, two daughters, and two rather spastic cats.

Visit her website at www.juliekenner.com to learn more and to connect with JK through social media!

CPSIA information can be obtained
at www.ICGtesting.com
Printed in the USA
LVHW041511111019
633943LV00011B/428/P

9 781949 925463